A Sydney Central Reunion

Welcome to Sydney Central Hospital!

Harper, Ivy, Alinta and Phoebe have reached the top at Sydney Central. Along the way, they've weathered the highs and lows of life but one thing has always remained steadfast: their friendship!

Now life's about to take an unexpected turn for the friends—it seems that Cupid has checked into Sydney Central Hospital!

Come and experience the rush of falling in love as these four feisty heroines meet their matches…

Harper and the Single Dad by Amy Andrews
Ivy's Fling with the Surgeon by Louisa George

Available now!

Ali and the Rebel Doc by Emily Forbes
Phoebe's Baby Bombshell by JC Harroway

Coming July 2023!

D1022825

Dear Reader,

When the editorial team approached myself, Emily Forbes, JC Harroway and Louisa George to write this quartet, it was a no-brainer. Our little Aussie/NZ contingent is a close one at the best of times but being able to work on a project with some of my best writer buds is always super fun. And getting to write such marvelously complex characters in a fantastic fictional setting we could make our own was the cherry on top.

Harper and Yarran have such a deliciously rich backstory it was a real treat to finally give them their much delayed happy ending. I hope you enjoy their reunion romance as much as I did writing it and enjoy glimpses of the other characters who will each get their HEA as the series unfolds.

Stay safe, take care and happy reading.

Love,

Amy xxx

HARPER AND THE SINGLE DAD

AMY ANDREWS

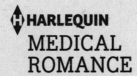

Special thanks and acknowledgment are given to Amy Andrews for her contribution to the A Sydney Central Reunion miniseries.

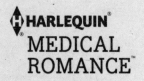

HARLEQUIN®
MEDICAL ROMANCE™

PLEASE RECYCLE
THIS PRODUCT IS RECYCLABLE

Recycling programs for this product may not exist in your area.

ISBN-13: 978-1-335-73792-2

Harper and the Single Dad

Copyright © 2023 by Harlequin Enterprises ULC

For questions and comments about the quality of this book, please contact us at CustomerService@Harlequin.com.

Harlequin Enterprises ULC
22 Adelaide St. West, 41st Floor
Toronto, Ontario M5H 4E3, Canada
www.Harlequin.com

Printed in U.S.A.

Amy Andrews is a multi-award-winning, *USA TODAY* bestselling Australian author who has written over fifty contemporary romances in both the traditional and digital markets. She loves good books, fab food, great wine and frequent travel—preferably all four together. To keep up with her latest releases, news, competitions and giveaways sign up for her newsletter, amyandrews.com.au.

Books by Amy Andrews

Harlequin Medical Romance

Visit the Author Profile page
at Harlequin.com for more titles.

I dedicate this book to my three coconspirators
in this quartet—Emily, JC and Louisa.
Thanks for the laughs, ladies xxx

CHAPTER ONE

HARPER JONES COULDN'T decide if it was a good thing or a bad thing to be thrown straight into a cardiac arrest on her first day as head of the emergency department at Sydney Central hospital. It would have been nice to get through all the introductions, at least. Meet the nurses and doctors, figure out who was who and who knew what and give a little spiel on her background and expectations.

But that wasn't how it worked in the ER.

When a walk-in collapsed at the front desk that was what you focused on instead of shaking hands and exchanging small talk. That was how it worked. And, an hour later, as the CCU team whisked the gravely ill patient away, Harper had come to know this group of people better than she could have at any polite meet and greet session.

She knew they were efficient and dedicated. She knew they were well-oiled and worked perfectly as a team. She knew their strengths and weaknesses.

Most importantly, she knew she'd fit in here. She'd made the right decision to leave London and finally come home.

'Dr Jones?'

Harper glanced up from the computer screen where she was completing paperwork for the cardiac arrest patient. 'Harper, please,' she corrected the nurse with a smile.

'Ambulance Control has just notified us of an incoming.' She glanced down at the paper in her hand. 'Emma Wilson, twenty six years old. Twenty-four weeks pregnant with twins. Burns from a house fire. Paramedics estimate twenty per cent with a mix of full and partial thickness.'

Something deep and dark twisted inside Harper at the word *fire* and her thoughts automatically went to the one man she'd been trying not to think about since arriving back in the country five days ago.

Yarran.

He still lived in Sydney. He was still a fireman. She hadn't deliberately kept tabs on him, but it was difficult not to know stuff in the age of social media and when Yarran was so entwined with her old friendship group. His twin sister, Alinta—older than him by five minutes—had been one of her closest friends, after all.

Before Harper had broken his heart twelve years ago, anyway…

But she couldn't think about that now. She couldn't think about how badly she'd screwed everything up and the bridges she had to repair. Because there was a pregnant woman suffering from significant burns who must be scared out of her wits. Harper's brain raced as she thought about how much more complicated the fluid resuscitation would be with two babies on board.

'She was trapped under some fallen debris and sustained legs burns,' the nurse—Taylor, according to her name tag—continued, oblivious to Harper's internal disquiet. 'She also has singeing around her nostrils and a soft stridor although she's sat'ting at one hundred per cent on a rebreather mask. ETA five minutes.'

Harper nodded, chewing on her bottom lip. *Stridor.* There were probably some inhalation burns with resultant airway swelling. Which meant they might need to tube her. Exactly *not* what was best for a pregnant woman.

'She's Aaron Wilson's wife,' Taylor added, and it was obvious from the nurse's tone the name should mean something. But it didn't.

'And he's someone I should know?'

'He's a TV celebrity. Front man for *If You Build It*—one of the most popular reality shows on television for people who fancy themselves as handy.'

'Ah, okay. Thanks.'

The premise sounded vaguely familiar given how much Australian TV content took up UK airwaves, but Harper had been a little too busy building her career to keep up with television. One thing she did know was that Aaron Wilson's celebrity could potentially complicate things for the hospital, as intense media interest often did.

'Is he accompanying her, did they say?'

There was no doubt a security protocol for this type of thing. At least Harper hoped so because the last thing she wanted was paparazzi in her ER, getting in the way.

'Apparently he's out of town but making his way back now.'

'Okay.' Hopefully Emma would be out of the ER before Aaron Wilson made an appearance and it would be the intensive care unit's problem. 'Where are we putting her?'

'Resus cube five.'

'Cool.' Harper nodded. 'I'll be there in one.'

Harper was putting on a plastic gown over her forest-green scrubs—the colour denoting medical staff—when she heard the first wails of the ambulance siren. Both the burns and obstetric team had been notified and were heading to the

ER and she was mentally preparing herself to come face to face with Alinta. Her ex-friend was, after all, head of the obs and gynae department so it was natural she would attend such a case.

A man in his thirties wearing smart trousers and a business shirt sans tie strode across the ER towards Harper. 'Hi,' he said as he approached. 'I'm Felix Rothbury, senior reg O & G.' He held out a hand. 'You must be Harper. Nothing like being thrown in at the deep end on the first day.'

Harper shook his hand automatically. 'Oh… hi. Sorry, I was expecting Ali.'

'Boss is filling in for a colleague who had to pull out of their presentation last moment at a maternal morbidity symposium in Canberra today. She'll be back tomorrow.'

A rush of relief flooded Harper's chest, which probably made her a terrible person and an even worse friend, but there it was. She *was* going to have to face Ali sometime as Ivy, another friend from Harper's past and Head of General Surgery, had pointed out this morning as they'd left Ivy's apartment, where Harper was staying temporarily.

Just not today. Not her *first* day.

'Fluid resus is going to be tricky,' he said, launching straight into logistics as the siren, which had grown louder and louder, suddenly stopped. The ambulance had obviously turned into the emergency vehicles entrance.

'Yeah.' Harper nodded. 'If you could assess what the babies are doing—' she tipped her chin at the ultrasound unit just outside the cubicle '—we can work with the burns team to figure out how to go forward.'

Because of the massive fluid shifts within the body in significant burns, it was imperative that fluids were replaced and intensely monitored. But this wasn't an ordinary burns case—they wouldn't be treating just one person, they'd be treating three. And if, as the nurse had suggested, the patient had inhalation burns requiring ventilation, then that was a whole other ball game.

If the pregnancy had been more advanced a caesarean would have been the first course of action, but no one was going to deliver twenty-four-week twins unless the mother's life was in immediate peril.

Hello, rock, meet hard place.

The ambulance-bay doors opened and two paramedics rushed their cargo inside. Harper's gaze flew to the woman on the stretcher. Emma's distressed cries could be heard easily from behind the plastic mask covering her nose and mouth even over the loud hiss of high-flow oxygen keeping the attached bag inflated. Her rounded belly was also obvious even below the shiny silver of the space blanket the paramedics had tucked around her to keep her warm.

The patient was wheeled into the cube, and the brakes applied. As the paramedics gave their handover, the team descended, seamlessly transferring the patient from the stretcher to the specially equipped resus bed before moving on to their assigned roles. The tank oxygen was switched over to the wall supply, Emma was hooked up to the cubicle monitor, the fluids currently running into two IVs placed in the crook of each elbow were switched to the hospital pumps, and baseline observations were recorded.

Harper concentrated on the information coming from the paramedic as the nurse in charge of the resus took position at the head of the stretcher and talked soothingly to the distressed patient, who was fretting about the babies. The professional, rapid-fire handover helped Harper mentally triage her priorities. The airway trumped everything. Then a full burns assessment was required and the fluid protocols for acute burns would be enacted. The condition of the babies needed to be ascertained.

And that was just for starters.

The crinkle of the space blanket being removed barely registered as the patient's legs were exposed. Whatever Emma had been wearing was now a mess of shredded fabric rucked up to her groin. Harper's gaze moved south inspecting the wet gauze dressings applied from mid thighs to toes, noting there didn't seem to be any circumferential involvement of the legs.

'I'm sorry but I need to get in there—'

Harper's gaze flicked to Felix and then to the fireman he was addressing. Engrossed as she'd been in her mental assessment and the paramedics' handover, Harper hadn't taken much notice of him there holding the patient's hand. Until now. Until he lifted his gaze to meet Harper's and for a few mad seconds everything stopped. A wild rushing filled her ears.

She knew that head with its thick, dark, wavy hair. And even with soot settling in the fine lines, she knew that face—the taut stretch of skin over that square jaw and those killer cheekbones. She knew that mouth with its two perfectly formed full lips. She knew those black-on-brown eyes, a little bloodshot though, as though it'd been a while since he'd slept. And full of compassion.

Yarran.

The years fell away and it was as if they'd never been apart. As if the last twelve years had never happened. Looking into those two deep, still pools now felt as it always had. There was such wisdom there. Wisdom not born of this time. And an incredible sense of self as well as a...*connection* to something much bigger.

A completely foreign concept to a girl who had grown up in the foster system.

If he was taken aback by seeing her, Harper couldn't tell. Unlike her own internal tumult, those eyes remained as calm and knowing as always and for those brief seconds she was twenty again and wanted nothing more than to drown in them.

But she wasn't twenty. And neither was he.

They were both forty and he had been married *and* widowed *and* had an almost-four-year-old since last she'd seen him. And she hadn't come home to rekindle anything. She hadn't come home for him, full stop. This was just the next step in her career.

And right now she had a patient who deserved her entire attention.

Dragging her eyes off him, Harper planted a trembling hand at the foot of the mattress as she mentally quashed the wash of emotion flooding every cell with a yawning kind of ache. She tamped it right down where everything else she'd ever dared feel had been hidden away, and tuned back into the handover.

'Sorry,' he said to Felix, his voice piercing her concentration more effectively than a bullet. 'I'll get out of your way.'

Given there were now seven medical personnel in the cubicle along with the bulky machine that was a no-brainer. Sure, everyone was gliding around each other in some bizarre medical ballet bringing a strange kind of fluidity to the chaos, but less, right now, was more.

The paramedics were still speaking but Harper found her eye drawn to Yarran as he leaned over and smiled at the woman on the stretcher, dwarfed in people and plastic and clearly scared out of her brain. 'I'm going to move out of the way now, Emma, so they can do their job.'

'No!' Emma's knuckles whitened as she gripped Yarran's hand tighter.

'Hey, it's okay,' he soothed. 'You're in good hands.'

'But you said—' Her voice broke on a sob as she pulled the mask away from her face. 'You said you wouldn't leave me.'

'I'm not leaving.' He patted her hand with a gentle patience so familiar to Harper it caused an almost violent gut clench. 'I'm just going to step outside so they can work but I'm not leaving. I'll come back in as soon as they tell me I can, and I won't leave until Aaron gets here.'

'You promise?' she demanded through more tears.

'I promise.'

Harper knew better than anyone that Emma could take that promise to the bank.

He left then, but not without a brief yet cataclysmic glance at Harper. One that seemed to say, *I've done my bit...now it's up to you.*

So...no pressure.

Harper mentally regrouped, pushing Yarran *freaking* Edwards from her mind. She had to, because Emma Wilson deserved a doctor on top of her game, not one dwelling on the past.

'How are the babies, Felix?' she asked, squeezing past to the head of the stretcher.

'Neither appear to be in distress,' he murmured, not lifting his gaze from the screen as he manipulated the probe with one hand and fiddled with buttons on the machine with the other. 'Both membranes are intact. Twin one's heart rate is slightly less than twin two's, but both are in healthy range. Good foetal movements.'

Okay. *Good.* For now, anyway. But Emma's stridor was a worry. 'Hi, Emma, I'm Harper Jones, the doctor in charge here today.'

Harper smiled confidently at her patient, who was looking flushed and wild-eyed. The paramedics had reported she'd refused anything for pain because she was worried about the effect on the babies, something that Emma reiterated as she pulled her mask aside again. 'Promise me you'll do everything you can to keep my babies safe?' she demanded in a husky voice.

Nodding, Harper gently returned the mask to Emma's face. 'Of course.'

But Harper knew the next couple of hours would be a tricky tightrope between doing what was best for Emma while trying to be as protective of her pregnancy as possible.

'You in pain?'

Emma shook her head. 'It's bearable,' she dismissed.

But Harper could see from the rigidity of her frame and the elevation of her blood pressure, she clearly *was* in pain. Which was, in a lot of ways, encouraging. Full thickness burns often weren't painful due to the depth of the injury, which hopefully meant that the majority of the burns were partial thickness. Emma would still need grafting, but they might be able to get away with doing less, which, given the pregnancy, would be preferable.

Just then a tall, lean guy with dark brown hair greying at the temples entered the cubicle followed by two women with stethoscopes slung around their necks. 'Hi,' he said. 'I'm Lucas Matthews. Head of Reconstructive Surgery.'

He appeared to be about forty and quite the looker, Harper supposed. The kind who naturally drew the female gaze and yet, she felt nothing. Not with the visceral pull of Yarran Edwards so fresh in her brain. But it was good to meet the surgeon who would be tasked with Emma's grafting.

'Harper Jones,' she replied. 'Are you happy to assess the thermal injuries while I keep on here?'

He plucked a pair of gloves out of the wall-mounted box. 'Sure thing.'

Harper returned her attention to her patient. 'Emma, I'm very worried about how noisy your breathing is. Sometimes when you're really close to a fire like you were, just breathing in the heat from it—as well as the smoke and sometimes the chemicals from whatever's burning around you—can cause damage to the mucous membranes lining the lungs and respiratory tract, which can cause them to swell. I think that noise I can hear when you breathe may be an indication of some swelling so I'm going to have a look and assess it.'

'Okay.' Emma nodded, her voice sounding husky now. 'What happens if there's swelling?'

Then they'd probably have to tube her before it got worse. Between the thermal injury and the significant amount of fluid she was about to receive, the tissues of her respiratory tract were going to take a hammering.

'It depends on the degree.' Harper wasn't

trying to be evasive but there was no point distressing Emma or getting too far ahead of themselves. 'Let me just have a look down your throat and we'll go from there.'

Two hours later they had stabilised Emma enough to get her transferred to the intensive care unit. There had been only slight redness of the upper airway so Harper hadn't needed to intubate but she suspected it would probably be required in the coming hours. Lucas had assessed the burns at twenty-five per cent—fifteen per cent of which were full thickness. Which meant extensive grafting.

Emma Wilson was here for the long haul.

Harper sent a swift prayer into the universe as the ICU team whisked a lightly sedated Emma away. After assurances from Felix that the babies were doing well and a small amount of pain relief would be fine, Emma had acquiesced. With it, her distress had settled, which had, in turn, settled her breathing and improved her stridor.

For now.

The Sydney Central was a top-notch hospital and Emma was in the best place possible but her pregnant body had also suffered a severe insult, which had the potential to get worse, jeopardising both her life and the babies' lives. Babies who were far too premature to be delivered and expected to survive. So, she was by no means out of the woods just yet. But she was at least settled for now, sleeping a little, giving her stress levels a much-needed break.

Stripping off her gloves, Harper tore the ties of her plastic gown and removed it, tossing it in a bin and heading for her office. She stopped dead in her tracks when she spotted Yarran sitting by himself in a row of four chairs in the corridor just outside the resus area, his head lolling back at an awkward angle against the wall.

Asleep.

A fascinating section of whiskery throat was exposed to her view and Harper felt a repeat of that moment back in the cubicle. That visceral gut clench. How was it possible he could affect her like this after twelve years apart?

Sighing, she approached—he'd get a crick in his neck if he stayed like that. Plus, she'd promised Emma she'd let Yarran know she was being transferred to ICU. Apparently, he'd been the one to pull her out from under the collapsed section of roof.

She'd called him her hero and looking at him now, oozing sheer masculinity even in his sleep, Harper agreed. Everything about him screamed big and capable. The guy who strode in when everything was burning down.

The guy who got it done.

From the tips of his soot-blackened, heavy work boots to the way his navy polo shirt stretched across his shoulders and abs, to the bands of reflective material encircling thighs and calves encased in thick navy trousers. Everything about him screamed 'hero'.

'Yarran.'

He didn't stir and Harper's heart did a little flip-flop behind her ribcage. Half of her wanted to let him sleep and the other half wanted to stroke her finger along the darkened shadow on his jawline and whisper his name as she used to.

As if they'd never been apart.

She wanted it so bad, her finger tingled in anticipation. But that wasn't going to happen. It could never happen.

They were so last decade.

Taking the safer route, Harper shook his arm, watching him as he stirred. He winced as he righted his head and cracked open an eye, looking at her in confusion for a moment or two before clarity returned. He stood abruptly, suddenly alert despite the overwhelming exhaustion stamped across his features.

'Emma?'

He was now significantly closer, looming in front of her and she could smell smoke but also something familiar, something that struck a chord deep in her reptilian brain. 'Just gone to ICU.'

He checked his watch. 'Has Aaron arrived?'

'He's apparently a few hours away.' It was then Harper noticed the congealed blood on the inner side of Yarran's forearm. She frowned. 'You're hurt.'

'Hmm? Oh—' He glanced at the injury, clearly annoyed it had the audacity to exist. 'It's nothing.'

'Why don't you let me be the judge of that?'

'It's fine,' he repeated, his tone testy. 'I need to get to ICU.'

Harper shook her head. 'Emma's sleeping at the moment and they won't let you in until they've got her settled anyway.'

'Is she going to be okay? Are the babies okay?'

Folding her arms, Harper raised an eyebrow. 'Let me look at that and I can fill you in on where she's at.'

He regarded her for a few moments. 'Fine.'

Yarran followed Harper into a treatment room still not quite able to believe she was here. He'd known she was back in the country. Known she'd taken the job at the Central. But he hadn't expected to run into her *ever* really, or not so soon, anyway. And certainly not on what was, according to the recent conversation he'd had with his twin, Ali, her first day.

He had given seeing Harper a brief thought sitting beside Emma in the ambulance but had dismissed it as fanciful. Surely her first day as department chief would involve a lot of meetings and HR stuff. Not being in the thick of an emergency right off the bat.

And certainly not attending to a lowly superficial scratch on his arm.

She flicked the lights on as she entered what was a typical hospital treatment room—cold, the bright white light making it seem even more so. The clinical aroma of antiseptic was pervasive yet comforting. Without a word, Harper pointed at the high, narrow bed pushed against the far wall and Yarran mentally apologised to the pristine white sheet as he levered his soot-covered ass onto the middle, his legs dangling over the edge.

They didn't speak. He just watched her gather the things she needed, in that quiet, efficient way of hers, as if they didn't have a whole truck full of baggage dominating the space between them. Her economy of movement hadn't changed in a decade. Nor had the shape of her body. Beneath those scrubs—she *still* looked good in scrubs— he could make out the leanness of her legs, the trimness of her frame, the high, tight thrust of her breasts.

His palms tingled as he remembered the feel of her under him and he pressed them to the bed. God…he must be tired to be thinking like this.

And he *was* tired. Actually, exhausted was probably a better word. Fatigue invaded every muscle cell he owned. His team had taken over at a factory fire when they'd come on shift last night and had spent seven hours getting it under control. Fighting a fire over a prolonged period was hot, sweaty work and manning a hose required extraordinary strength. Doing so for hours, even more so.

Then, two hours before the shift was due to end, they'd been called to the Wilsons' house fire. It hadn't taken long to get under control but the adrenaline that came with a suburban fire took its own kind of toll. Unlike the abandoned warehouse, the potential for people being trapped and the fire spreading to neighbouring properties was ever present.

So yeah, he felt weary to his bones. He stunk of smoke and was streaked with soot. His eyes were gritty from ash and fumes and weariness. He wanted a shower and he wanted his bed. He did not want to be here with Harper Jones staring back into a past he suddenly wasn't sure now he was as over as he'd thought.

Turning, she pushed a metallic trolley laden with dressing equipment towards him. She halted close enough that the outside of her thigh brushed the outside of his knee as she snapped on a pair of gloves. A flare of heat flashed up his quad and the fatigued muscle protested the involuntary tightening. Harper didn't look similarly affected as she held out her hand, clearly expecting him to present his arm.

Yarran sighed. 'It really is fine.' But she just stood there, implacable as ever. Implacable as that night she'd turned his proposal down.

Sliding her hand onto his forearm, she flipped it over so she could examine the underside then lifted it slightly to examine it closer. Yarran didn't resist—he didn't have the energy. Although clearly his body wasn't *that* tired as a warm buzz flushed through his system at her touch.

'What happened?' she asked with such brisk efficiency Yarran was left in no doubt he was the only one feeling the buzz.

'I don't really remember. I think it might have been when my shirt caught on something as I pulled Emma out from the debris.'

She lifted her gaze and their eyes met and locked and Yarran was conscious of how close they were, of how easy it would be to slide a hand onto her hip, to tug her near and bury his face in her neck. She smelled so good and looked so fresh and so...*here*. After all this time. It had been over a decade and yet it felt like yesterday.

'You didn't feel anything? It must have hurt.'

Yarran shrugged. 'Nope.' It wasn't unusual in the midst of a fire or a rescue, with adrenaline surging, to sustain a minor injury or burn and not even know it.

Their gazes held for a beat or two, her hazel eyes familiar to him on such an intimate level. How many times had he stared into those eyes as they'd chatted about their days, their plans, their future?

How many times had he stared into them as they'd made love?

She quirked an eyebrow at his brief response. 'People come into emergency departments demanding morphine for papercuts.'

He shrugged again. 'I didn't feel it.'

Shaking her head, she dropped her gaze back to his wound and set about thoroughly cleaning the area. As promised, she filled him in on Emma's injuries and condition with a brisk, businesslike demeanour that helped keep this moment in perspective.

Once all the soot and dried blood had been removed it was, as he suspected, a superficial cut *not* requiring any medical intervention. Still, he had to grit his teeth a little as she scrubbed directly at the ten-centimetre laceration with an anti-bacterial solution. He grunted as she swabbed it again.

'Sorry.' She glanced at him quickly. 'Don't want it to get infected.'

'Not much danger of that,' Yarran grouched. 'My arm's never been cleaner.'

Ignoring his grumpiness, she returned her attention to his arm, inspecting it carefully. 'Okay, it's just a superficial cut.'

Yarran rolled his eyes as he stared at the curve of her cheekbone and the half-moon shadow created by her eyelashes. 'Yeah.'

She released his arm, reaching for a wound dressing. 'I'll just pop a dressing over it.'

Yarran sat passively as she applied it, taking her time adhering the sticky edges to his skin, working out a wrinkle from a section daring to not sit perfectly. It was torturous, cool her fingertips trailing against the flesh of his inner arm, light and cool, sensation curling upwards his arm, light as smoke.

A slice of her hair fell forward. It was still the same vibrant red as always, no sign of any greys to dull its glory. She wore it shorter, though, the tips brushing her shoulders rather than her waist, but it looked as lush and soft as always and he was shocked by the sudden urge to sink his hands into it, to feel the glide of it as it sifted through his fingers, to bury his face in it.

To see it fanned over the pillow beside his.

Something deep and hard kicked him in the chest and he started. Fifteen minutes ago, all he'd wanted was a shower and his bed and now he wanted…what? To…rekindle something with the woman who had smashed his heart into a thousand tiny pieces?

He hadn't wanted anybody for a long time. And now this? With *Harper*?

'There now,' she said, oblivious to his inner turmoil, her eyes meeting his. 'You want a lollipop?'

A smile played on her mouth and lit those hazel eyes. The same hazel eyes that had clouded over when he'd dropped to his knee and proposed all those years ago.

What are you doing, Yarran? Get up, please, just get up.

He still remembered that moment. The look of horror on her face, the icy cold fingers wrapping around his heart and squeezing. He'd been so sure. *So sure* of her and how she felt. That she wanted the same thing he did—a life together. He remembered the heavy pain in his chest as his heart had cleaved right down the centre.

And then she'd bolted—to the other side of the planet—leaving Yarran dead inside. So dead he'd never thought he'd feel anything again. And he hadn't—for a long time. Then Marnie had come along six years ago and breathed life back into him. He'd loved again and when they'd had their son—Jarrah—Yarran had felt complete.

But then Marnie had been so cruelly taken from him in a car accident just after Jarrah's first birthday and his world had turned bleak. *So bleak.* Thank goodness for Jarrah. His son had given him reason to keep going.

Reason to laugh and feel joy again and he'd clung to that.

It had been a long process, but he was finally in a good place. He had a kid he adored, a job he loved and a supportive family. He didn't *need* anything else.

Hell, he didn't *want* anything else.

He certainly didn't want to go backwards. And Harper was the very definition of backwards. Yarran was a different person today. Not the same guy who fell so quickly and trusted so easily. And he had responsibilities now. He had Jarrah. And Jarrah came first.

'Yarran?'

Her husky voice brought him back to this moment. This woman so familiar yet so *not*. So close. *Too close.* Frowning at him, her brow crinkled, those eyes searching his, everything around them coming to a stop. The busy emergency ward noises in the corridor fading. The breath in his lungs stuttering to a halt. The trip of his heart pausing.

He was conscious only of her—of her breathing and the aroma of her hair. Of the hot lick of desire throbbing to life inside him. His gaze dropped to Harper's mouth and the urge to kiss the hell out of her rode him like the devil.

She swallowed. *'Yarran.'*

Her voice was low and rough, husky with warning. One he would do well to heed but now he was caught up by the fascinating bob of her throat, the flutter of her pulse at the base, the memory of kissing her there so many times. How good it had been.

Until it wasn't.

Panic flooded in then, riding shotgun with his desire. Hell. What was he thinking? This was Harper. *Harper.* He wasn't thinking. At all. He was tired—so tired—and seeing her again after all this time was a shock.

Yarran stood abruptly, forcing Harper to take a step back. 'I've got to go,' he said gruffly, manoeuvring around her stationary body. 'I promised Emma I wouldn't leave her.'

He wasn't asking for her permission and he didn't wait for it, he just walked out of the room, not looking back, refusing to think about how close he'd come to doing something so incredibly stupid. His body might be caught up in a time warp, but his head was not.

There could be no do-overs with Harper Jones.

CHAPTER TWO

A FEW HOURS LATER, Harper was standing in line at Perc Up, the café bar over the road from the hospital. It was obviously popular given the size of the queue and she could see why. Big windows looked out on the busy road while, overhead, myriad bare light bulbs clung to the ceiling Hollywood-mirror style. Multiple comfy-looking faux chesterfield lounges in buttery leather faced each other over worn Turkish-style rugs.

The view through the glass was partially obscured by creeping vines that spilled from pots sitting on shelves affixed above the windows and real potted palms—not plastic—sat on multiple surfaces throughout. They were large and lush, their leaves showy and tropical, and Harper had no doubt she'd have admired the décor a hell of a lot more on a different day.

Just not this day. Several hours after the shock of seeing Yarran again so soon and that *almost kiss.* Because she had no doubt that was where it had been heading…

It was all just too much to process today on top of two emergency cases in quick succession. How could there still be such an intense *thing* between them? Because he'd obviously felt it, too. It had been *twelve* years, for Pete's sake. They'd both moved on. They weren't the twenty-year-olds they'd been when they'd first got together. She'd had several liaisons since—although none serious—and he'd *married*, for God's sake.

He had a kid.

'Hey, you.'

Harper started at the sound of Ivy's voice but was inordinately grateful she was here dragging Harper out of circuitous thoughts. 'Hey.'

'I hear your first day got off to a real bang.'

Dr Ivy Hurst had formed part of Harper's tight friendship circle back in the day, along with Ali and Phoebe Mason. They'd all met in med school and, much to Harper's surprise, had all clicked. She wasn't sure what they saw in her—Harper Jones, the outsider—but she was exceedingly grateful these women had been patient with her reticence and drawn her in, holding her close when her instincts had always been set to flee.

'You could say that.'

'How's the burns patient?'

Harper filled Ivy in on the case as the queue moved closer to the counter. 'I rang ICU just before I came over and her airway swelling had started to get markedly worse so they've tubed her.' Harper shook her head. 'The pregnancy complicates everything drastically.'

Ivy nodded, her caramel hair swishing. She was shorter and curvier to Harper's taller, sportier figure. 'True. But she has the best damn multi-disciplinary team in the country working around the clock to give her and the babies the best care. And, it could have been worse. A ceiling collapse in a house fire?' Ivy shuddered. 'She was lucky to get out alive.'

Which brought Yarran squarely back into Harper's thoughts. Looking all big and broad and sooty. And tired. So tired. Yet, so damn *good*.

'Yeah.'

'Hey.' Ivy snapped her fingers in front of Harper's face. 'Where'd you go?'

'Sorry.' Harper grimaced. 'I—'

She shook her head, contemplating whether to tell Ivy about Yarran. Harper's early years had taught her to be self-reliant, even secretive, so it had never felt natural to blurt out personal stuff. Then she'd become friends with Ivy, Ali and Phoebe and learned it was okay to share things with your besties.

They listened, they commiserated, they advised. And they never ever judged.

It had been over a decade since they'd shared that dynamic, but Harper had been hoping, with her return, it could be rekindled. So maybe this was a good place to start.

'I…ran into Yarran.'

The expression on Ivy's face was almost comical *'What? Shut up!'*

Harper laughed; she couldn't help it. 'Nope. He came in holding Emma's hand.'

Ivy fluttered her hand over her chest in a hubba-hubba way. 'Of course he did. That man, honourable as the day is long and, Lordy…forty looks *good* on him.'

Harper couldn't have agreed more as Ivy's gaze turned speculative. 'How was it?'

Intense. Cataclysmic. Unsettling. 'Weird.'

'Bad weird, or—' she waggled her eyebrows '—good weird.'

'There's a good weird?'

'With old boyfriends? Sure.' She waved at the air as if the question was a no-brainer. 'Was there some residual…*somethin'-somethin'*?'

Oh, yeah, there'd been that—with bells on. But Harper wasn't ready to share that just yet. She was barely processing it herself. 'Are you forgetting I rejected his marriage proposal and broke his heart twelve years ago? *And* he'd been married and widowed in the interim?'

'Sure.' Another air-wave. 'But…if there was a little *weakening* below the belly button, then what?'

The question hung in the air, tantalising in ways Harper didn't want to either acknowledge or understand. 'Ali would have my guts for garters.' She'd been furious at Harper's rejection of Yarran.

That whole 'twins feeling each other's pain' thing was *real*.

'Right. Which is why we need to get the gang back together.' Ivy held up a hand to still Harper as she opened her mouth to object. 'I know you wanted to get settled into your own apartment before reconnecting with Ali beyond any hospital interactions but, hon, that's just not going to work now. Yarran is for damn sure going to tell Ali you guys met because they tell each other everything.'

Ivy was right. And Harper did want to reconnect with her old friends. She'd love to be able to get back to what they had been. She'd *missed* her friends. She'd missed *Ali*.

Smart, passionate, protective, loyal Ali.

Ivy, obviously sensing Harper wavering,

moved in for the kill. 'There's a lot to be said for ripping the plaster off, hon.'

She sighed. 'Yep…okay, sure.'

'Yes—reunion dinner!' Ivy did a little body shimmy. 'Friday night. Phoebe's back from her conference by then and we can strike while the iron is hot.' She happy sighed. 'It'll be like old times, just you wait and see.'

Harper nodded and smiled, not wanting to dampen Ivy's enthusiasm, but she figured it'd probably be a while before it felt like old times. Except of course for Yarran. Her body was firmly in old times territory where he was concerned. Remembering every kiss and touch, every magical minute.

Great. Just great…

It was six in the evening before Harper got away. As first days went, it was one for the books and she was looking forward to a shower and kicking back with Ivy when she was through with her rounds. Walking across the spacious lobby, she admired the towering glass atrium showcasing the last streaks of sunlight gilding the clouds vibrant oranges and reds.

The architecturally designed hospital had won awards for its use of glass to amplify the space and light and Harper made a mental note to go up to the renowned rooftop gardens and watch the sunset some time soon. But right now, a shower was calling.

She slowed as she approached the bank of lifts, suddenly noticing a clutch of what she assumed were media cordoned off beyond the front entrance, if the presence of zoom lenses and a hovering security guard was anything to go by.

Anybody would think they were harbouring a new royal baby inside.

The hospital had issued a standard *no comment* in a media release several hours ago—as had Aaron's management—but that hadn't stopped a pack of hungry reporters descending.

She'd heard a very harried Aaron Wilson had run the gauntlet of them as he'd swept into the hospital half an hour ago and it seemed as though they were now camping out for the duration.

Absently she registered the lift dinging and, as she drew level, the doors opened and Yarran strode out almost directly in her path. They didn't crash but they were both forced to stop abruptly and then they just stared at each other for what felt like a lot longer than the probable few seconds it actually was.

He'd washed up a little, his face now free of sooty streaks, but she could still smell smoke and that vaguely familiar aroma she couldn't put her finger on. His wavy hair looked as though it had been finger-combed for hours. The curls were in total disarray and, for a crazy second, Harper wanted to push her hands into the dark silky mass and brush it back into place.

Except she couldn't move. Not when his eyes roved, holding her firmly in place. They travelled from her hair to her face then down over the fit of her scrubs, his gaze hungry and heated as if he were seeing her for the first time again after her long absence from his life.

Harper felt the rawness of it—the urgency—in every cell. In the catch of her breath, the clench of her stomach and the wild flutter of her pulse at the base of her throat. A pulse he noticed, his gaze zeroing in, her nipples hardening at the intense sexuality of his scrutiny.

'You're still here?' Harper said, finally finding her voice as she tore herself back from the frighteningly intense draw of him.

'Yeah.' He cleared his throat as though the effort to pull himself back had been difficult too. 'Aaron's with Emma now so...'

'You're not on shift tonight?'

'No. I have a couple of days off now.'

The front entrance sliding doors opened, admitting some hospital staff along with the calls from the press, who clearly thought anyone in uniform was fair game to share insider information on the Wilsons. The click of the cameras echoed around the atrium like gunfire.

'Ugh,' Harper muttered. 'That looks like fun. *Not.*'

The last thing she wanted was to have to brave that lot. She glanced at Yarran, who was obviously going to be a prime target with the fire service emblem embroidered on the pocket of his T-shirt and the high-vis piping around his legs.

'You ready to gird your loins?' she asked and then immediately wished the floor would open up and swallow her.

Do not mention the man's loins, idiot.

Thankfully Yarran left it alone as his expression turned grim. 'No way.' He shook his head. 'Come on. I know another way out of here.'

She supposed he did—his sister worked here and, apart from the fact he'd probably been to the ER frequently over the years, she knew part of the fire service's job was knowing the layout of city hospitals in case of evacuation. But she hadn't been prepared for him to grab her hand as he did as he turned on his heel and tugged.

Harper followed without comment, too aware of him and their intimate hold to risk conversation. She just lengthened her stride to keep pace and, before she knew it, he was dragging her through the bottom of the fire escape. Ignoring the stairs, he strode across the well to the door on the other side and pushed it open.

They stepped out into a wide, clean alley that appeared to be some kind of service corridor, if the nearby forklift was any indication. But, more importantly, it was blissfully free of media. It was only then that he let go of her hand.

'Thank you,' she said, her voice ridiculously husky, her palm tingling as she became aware she was alone with him—again.

Which was dumb—they were in an *alley*, for God's sake. There was heavy machinery six feet away. It was hardly intimate. And yet the gentle kiss of twilight seemed to bathe the area in a romantic deep lavender glow.

'Are you in the car park?'

'Yes.' She nodded. 'What about you?'

'I'll get an Uber.'

Of course. He'd have come to the hospital in the back of an ambulance. 'I can drop you back to your station to pick up your car?'

She had no idea where his fire station was these days and probably being alone with him in a car wasn't wise, but it seemed churlish not to offer—they *had* been friends once, for crying out loud. And if she and Ali were ever going to get close again, Harper needed to accept Yarran was going to be back in her life, too.

Which meant they had to find some kind

of way to get beyond their past. A way to be friends. Like giving him a lift back to the station. Friends gave each other lifts, right?

'Nah, it's fine.' He shook his head. 'I got the bus into work last night. It's easy to grab an Uber.'

If Sydney Ubers were anything like London's during peak hour there'd be some ridiculous surcharging going on. She had no doubt he could afford an Uber, but it didn't seem right letting him do it when she could easily drop him home. 'Or…' she smiled '… I could just drop you home.'

'I live in Sunrise Bay.'

'I know.'

His eyes widened a little. 'You been keeping tabs on me, Harper?'

There was a gravelly undertone to the enquiry that sent Harper's pulse fluttering again, which made her irritable.

Enough already!

'Well, I don't know your *exact* address or anything, but I am Facebook friends with your sister,' she said waspishly, 'and while I've been too busy building my career to endlessly scroll social media like most people on the planet, I've seen enough here and there to gather you live near your parents.'

'Right.' He conceded with a small smile. 'Which is the opposite direction to Ivy's.'

So, he knew she was staying with Ivy… Harper quirked an eyebrow. '*You* been keeping tabs on *me*?' The only social media she was on was Facebook, and Harper never posted anything. She barely ever looked at her feed.

He shrugged. 'I overhead Ali mentioning it to Mum.'

'Ah.' Harper nodded absently, undecided whether she was okay that Yarran *hadn't* been keeping tabs on her. 'Well…anyway…' She shook herself out of her contemplation. 'I'm perfectly fine to drive you twenty minutes to Sunrise Bay.'

He regarded her solemnly for a beat or two, his lips pursed as if he was weighing up all the pros and cons, and she had to stop herself from rolling her eyes. Once upon a time, Yarran had been spontaneous. That was one of the many things she'd loved about him. So different from her and her cautious approach to life. But, she supposed, not a lot had gone according to plan for Yarran so she could hardly blame him.

'Okay.' He nodded slowly. 'Thank you.'

They sat in silence as Harper manoeuvred her rental out of the hospital car park. The radio was came on once they were out of the parking garage and Yarran seemed content to listen as he stared out of the window. He didn't even give directions. Not that she needed them—not yet anyway. It might have been over a decade since she'd lived in Sydney but she still remembered how to get to Sunrise Bay.

Once upon a time the Edwards house had felt like hers as she, Ali, Phoebs and Ivy spent many a night cramming for uni exams there, being kept in carbs and caffeine by Ali's mother. And then, as she and Yarran became a thing, spending nights and staying weekends.

Feeling loved and included. Almost feeling like one of them.

As though she almost belonged. But not ever really trusting that she could have it all.

Constantly on tenterhooks as the years passed and chatter about weddings and *babies* grew louder. Wanting Yarran but too scarred from her past to trust—not in him, but in herself. Living with the constant slick undercurrent of panic. Waiting for the moment it would all come crashing down. When it would all end and she'd have to leave.

Because that was better than being left.

So when the opportunity came up to go to London, it had been perfect. Harper had jumped at it. How was she to know Yarran had picked the very night she was going to tell him about moving to the other side of the world to propose?

'Who looks after your son?' she asked into the growing silence. Anything to take her mind off that night. 'When you're at work.'

'Jarrah.' He turned his head to look at her. 'His name is Jarrah.'

Harper nodded, her hands gripping the steering wheel a little tighter. Jarrah. Yarran's *son*. Harper hadn't ever wanted kids—apart from a couple of blissful years with a great-aunt, she'd had no motherly role models to speak of—but as her relationship with Yarran had continued his parents had started mentioning grandkids.

Yarran's children. With Yarran's dark eyes and his dark curly hair and his beautiful brown skin. And that had added to the panic.

'Does he have a nanny or childcare or…?'

'A little bit of everything, really. Like most single parents it's a bit of a juggle and between kindy and after-school care, as well as Ali and Mum and Dad, I have a village helping me. He's been at Mum and Dad's the last few days. They take him when I work nights or weekends.'

'You're lucky to have them.'

He gave a half-laugh. 'Don't I know it. I wouldn't have managed without them after…'

Yarran looked back out of the window without finishing his sentence. He didn't need to. Harper knew what he'd been about to say—*after my wife died*. And it gave her a perfect opportunity to do what she should have done three years ago. 'I'm so sorry about your wife…about Marnie. I sent a condolence card.'

And she'd felt crappy about it. She should have picked up the phone, talked to him, but so many years had passed and there'd been no contact and she hadn't known what to say. Sorry had seemed so inadequate. So, she'd chickened out.

'I got it. Thank you.'

Harper wanted to say more. Wanted to ask more. About her. About Marnie. The woman Yarran had loved after he'd stopped loving her. She hadn't been jealous or upset he'd moved on; in fact, she'd felt a strange kind of kinship with this other woman. Yarran was one of the best people she'd ever known—one of the good guys—and Harper had been grateful to her. And relieved and happy Yarran had been able to move on.

Unlike her.

But she didn't speak. She didn't ask the questions pushing at the back of her throat. There'd been a bleak kind of finality to his voice and his body language was saying *don't*.

Maybe just seeing each other again was enough for one day.

So they remained silent until she turned into Sunrise Bay and Yarran directed her to his place. Harper inspected it as she pulled up outside—neat, two storeys, brick, with beautifully landscaped gardens bordering a manicured lawn. She'd bet there was a big backyard and probably a pool.

'How long have you lived here?' she asked as he made no move to get out and the silence weighed hot and heavy against her.

'A few years. It was easier to be closer to Mum and Dad with Jarrah.'

She nodded. 'It looks lovely.'

'Yeah.' Yarran glanced up at the building. 'We like it. Poor Wally didn't know what to do with himself though, when we moved in. All that space in the backyard after a tiny square of grass at the old place.'

Harper blinked. *Wally?* Her gaze landed on his profile. 'Wally's still alive?'

Yarran turned his head and their gazes met. 'Yep. Fourteen years and still kicking.'

They'd plucked Wally, a four-month-old chocolate Labrador, out of the shelter a couple of years before Harper had left. It had been love at first sight for all three of them and leaving the doggo behind had been just one of the many wrenches of her move.

'He has some arthritis now, which makes him

a little slower, but he can still open the fridge when you're not looking and he's very protective of Jarrah.'

Another stupid lump lodged in Harper's throat. 'I assumed… I didn't know… Wow.'

'Yeah.' Then he smiled and Harper wasn't prepared for it. Cheekbones and dimples, she thought absently. It wasn't fair the man should be blessed with both. 'You want to come up and see him?'

This was one of those times when Harper knew she should definitely say no. Those dimples alone were a blaring foghorn and there'd already been a *lot* today. That near-kiss moment in the treatment room a warning shot across the bow.

But… *Wally*!

She smiled back and switched off the engine. 'I'd love to.'

Harper walked through the front door as Yarran pushed it open and indicated she should precede him. She caught a waft of something familiar again as she brushed past tempting her to linger but she didn't, walking straight into an open-plan living, dining and kitchen area.

Warm downlights glowed from the ceiling, bathing wooden floorboards in soft yellow light. At the far side was a bank of floor-to-ceiling sliding doors, which led out onto a deck lit by a string of fairy lights entwined around the railings.

It was homely, with comfy patchwork couches, and a corner piled high with transparent plastic tubs of toys. A big-screen TV hung from the wall opposite the three-seater couch, where several stuffed toys were discarded. A large wooden coffee table sat just in front of the couch with several toy trains sitting on top. A train track, complete with stations and signals, looped around the base.

'This is nice,' she said as the door clicked shut and Yarran moved past her, heading for the kitchen.

'Thanks. We like it.'

Harper followed him slowly inside as he placed his keys and mobile phone on the bench top before turning to open the fridge door. 'You want something to drink? Tea? Coffee? A glass of wine?'

She halted on the other side of the central island bench. *Wine?* The last thing she needed right now, with his back view looking just as fine as his front, was to have her inhibitions lowered. Being in his home, getting an insight into what his life had been without her, felt confronting enough without alcohol.

The sweet ache of nostalgia mixed with a

heavier feeling of regret to form an unholy alliance, needling at her skin.

'No. Thanks.'

He reached for the carton of juice and turned back to her, lifting it to his mouth and drinking it straight from the carton, his Adam's apple bobbing, his eyelids sweeping shut. He'd always done that and, instead of finding it annoying like his mother, Harper had found it utterly freaking masculine. And strangely erotic.

As if his thirsts weren't easily contained by manners and propriety.

His eyes fluttered open and Harper's breath stuttered to a halt as their gazes met. It was only for a couple of beats but long enough for her heart to bump against her ribs and for her thighs to tremble and her nipples to tighten.

Hell, Harper couldn't believe her scrubs weren't smouldering.

A dog barked then and Harper dragged herself back from the pit of quicksand she'd been circling. Back to the present. To their baggage. To the stick-figure crayon drawing behind Yarran's head that was fixed to the fridge with a *best daddy ever* magnet.

Yarran was not the same person he'd been twelve years ago. And neither was she.

Her pulse loud in her ears, Harper turned to

the sliding doors to find another piece of her past squirming his body towards her. 'Wally!'

Tossing her car keys on the island top, she strode towards the dog and had the door open within seconds, much to Wally's delight. She dropped to her knees and hugged him tight, a wall of emotion lodging in her throat and pricking at the backs of her eyes.

'I can't believe it's you, Wally.' She sighed contently then laughed as he shimmied his entire body in her arms, making it impossible to hold him properly.

Harper sensed Yarran coming closer and Wally barked happily at his master as he madly wagged his tail and wriggled on the spot. Yarran laughed. 'I know, boy.' He scratched behind Wally's ears and the dog's eyes rolled back in ecstasy. 'She's back.'

She's back.

Two little words stabbing into her soul. Had he known she would be? Had he wanted it? Had he lain in bed at night, yearning for her the way she'd yearned for him?

Giving herself a mental shake, Harper glanced up from the greyed muzzle of Wally the wonder dog, as they used to call him. 'You think he recognises me?'

'Yeah.' Yarran's steady look pierced through

her as he continued to show Wally some love. 'I do.'

Harper never had a pet growing up so she wasn't familiar with dog stuff. 'It's been so long. I…figured he'd forget me.'

'You're a lot of things, Harper Jones, but forgettable is not one of them.'

She swallowed at the gravelly pitch to his voice. He hadn't forgotten her. Just as she hadn't forgotten him. No matter how much she'd told herself she had.

Told herself she *should*.

Breaking eye contact again, she sank down and Wally shimmied into another squirmy hug. Shutting her eyes, Harper held him tight, the press of his wriggly body bombarding her with a hundred memories. She was conscious of Yarran standing over her, conscious of an ache, of a restlessness that fizzed between them in a purely sexual way.

And she suddenly couldn't take any more. Her system was in nostalgia overload and she had to get out. 'I've gotta go.' She stood abruptly, heading for the kitchen.

'Harper.'

Ignoring him, she passed between the island and the bank of kitchen cupboards against the wall to fetch her keys, which had slid across the surface when she'd tossed them there. Taking a breath she said, 'Thank you,' then turned slightly to acknowledge him—it would be rude not to, after all.

Except she'd thought he'd still be over with Wally. But he wasn't. Wally was outside, looking in through the screen door, and Yarran was behind her. Right there. So close. And looking all big and broody and so… *God*…so good. And she wanted to walk into his arms and lay her cheek on his chest as she'd done so many times before, but she couldn't because she'd screwed it all up. The thought caught like a burr in her throat and Harper blinked back a well of stupid tears.

His expression softened as he took a step closer. 'Harper…'

Harper's pulse thrummed frantically at her temple. 'I'm fine.'

But she wasn't because he was so near and she'd missed him so much. *So much*. Why had she underestimated how hard it would be to see him again?

Slowly, he shook his head. 'I don't think you are.'

Then he took another step, his hand reaching for her, his palm sliding onto the side of her neck, his fingers gliding into the hair at her nape, his thumb drifting lazily across the angle of her jaw.

'Harper,' he murmured, his head lowering, his gaze scorching her mouth.

Her name rumbled from his lips and every pulse point keened to his touch. Her breathing constricted as a low throb—hot and slick—flared to life between her legs. But still, she *could* have pulled back, *could* have stepped away. She could have stopped this.

She just didn't want to.

When his mouth touched down it was soft and tentative and she sighed against his lips as if she'd been waiting for this moment from the second their eyes had met again in the ER. The lightest of brushes and yet every part of her melted as she swayed towards him and he swayed towards her, their bodies *just* skimming—thighs, hips, chests—while her heart just about thumped out of her chest.

He tasted tangy like orange juice as she breathed in the aroma of him—smoke and that familiar back note that had been bugging her all day except now she knew what it was. *Acqua di Gio.*

She'd bought him his first ever bottle.

'God,' he muttered, pulling back enough for Harper to see his eyes clouded with lust and confusion. 'It's like you never went away.'

Then he kissed her again and made a noise at the back of his throat so damn urgent and needy and...*feral* it exploded through her body in a flash of white-hot light and the kiss went from tentative to explosive.

From zero to nuclear in one beat of her heart.

His hand jerked her closer, their bodies locked tight now as she clung to him, drowning in lust and Acqua Di Gio. Yarran's mouth grew hotter and harder and more demanding and Harper met him at every turn and twist, inhaling noisily as she shifted restlessly against the hard planes of his body trying to get closer.

Trying to *get inside* him.

He moved slightly and suddenly she was trapped between the hardness of his body and the immovability of the benchtop, her nipples a hot ache as they rubbed against his chest. Then he slid a thick thigh between her legs, pressing against the scream of nerves at the apex, and she thrust her hands into his hair, twisting her fingers hard. He grunted at the bite but Harper was too far gone to care as she whispered, *'Yarran,'* urgently against his mouth.

The jangle of his phone sliced through the red-hot veil of Yarran's lust like a machete. It was his mother's ringtone and he jerked out of the kiss as if he'd been hit by a cattle prod, his pulse thudding through his neck, his chest, his groin. His breathing as erratic as Harper's.

Yarran stared at her for a beat. He'd done that. He'd made her noisily drag air in and out and her mouth all wet and puffy. He'd put that hazy sheen of lust in her eyes. He was responsible for her bewildered expression. The way she'd twisted her fingers in his hair when he'd pushed between her legs…

And, hell, if that hadn't rushed to his head at a dizzying speed.

'That's Mum,' he said as the ringing continued, his voice weirdly husky. 'I've got to get it.' Yarran had rung his mother earlier to explain where he was and ask her to pick up Jarrah from school and keep him at theirs for a while longer.

He hadn't mentioned seeing Harper again. No, he didn't know why.

Harper nodded as if she was unable to form coherent words and Yarran couldn't help but feel a stab of male satisfaction. Her breath caught as he eased his thigh from between hers and, hell, if he didn't want to ignore the damn phone and jam his leg right back in there.

Rub and grind against her. Hear her call out his name again as if she couldn't get enough of him, as if they'd never been apart.

He stepped away instead and reached for the phone.

'Hi, Mum,' he said as he answered it, leaning his butt against the counter and watching Harper as she moved away, sliding her hands onto the bench opposite, her back to him.

'Hi, darling. Just ringing to check if you're back from the hospital yet and want us to bring Jarrah around or should we keep him another night so you can crash?'

Harper turned then, lust still lingering in her eyes, and he had to grind his feet into the floor to stop from tossing the phone and putting his mouth back where it belonged. 'Just got home,' he said, fighting an internal battle against the temptation his mother was offering.

There wasn't one part of him that didn't know he and Harper could pick right back up where they'd left off. There wasn't one part of him that didn't want it, either.

'Bring him over whenever you're ready.'

It wasn't great parenting to put his kid between him and temptation but, right now, it was all he had. Because this thing between him and Harper today was madness. It was nostalgia and muscle memory—and he would do well to remember Harper had run from a commitment twelve years ago when there'd only been him.

And it wasn't just him any more.

Maybe she was different now but he couldn't risk his heart again, not when he had Jarrah to consider. Jarrah, who had already lost one important woman from his young life.

Yarran didn't have the luxury of being young and stupid any more, pinning his hopes on someone he'd always known, on some deep visceral level, had one eye on the door.

He'd just been so certain she loved him more than her insecurities and he could love her enough to make her stay.

Hanging up from his mother, he glanced at Harper. 'Jarrah will be home soon.'

She nodded and cleared her throat and Yarran watched the last vestiges of their passion clear from her eyes. 'Of course.' She pushed off the bench. 'I'll be on my way.'

'Wait.' Yarran held up his hand and she stopped. 'Let's go out for a drink on Saturday night.'

A frown knitted her brows together. 'I don't think that's wise, do you?'

'Look.' Yarran shoved a hand through his hair. 'You're back. And we're going to run into each other. Between our jobs and Ali, it's inevitable. So...let's clear some air, talk about what happened twelve years ago, get it out in the open. I think half the problem today was that we've never talked. And maybe if we did, we could finally put it and any residual feelings behind us and get on with our lives. Hell, maybe we can become friends, Harper. We used to be friends...'

For about three seconds anyway. Before their attraction took over.

She nodded slowly. 'It would make things easier with Ali if we were friends.'

'Okay. Good. What's your number? I'll text you the details.'

Yarran tapped in the number as she reeled it off then she scooped up her keys and, without looking back, headed for the door. He wondered, as he watched her go, if seeing her walk away ever got easier?

CHAPTER THREE

'NERVOUS?'

Harper nodded as butterflies fluttered in her belly. 'A little,' she acknowledged as she and Ivy walked to Ali's apartment near the hospital Friday night. Seeing Yarran had been hard but unexpected so there'd been no time to work herself into a tizz.

As she was now.

The prospect of facing Ali again was *nerveracking*. They'd been close once—as close as it was possible for Harper to be to anyone, anyway—and she'd messed it all up and she knew Ali blamed her for breaking Yarran's heart. She knew because hot-headed Ali had told her in a confrontation the day before Harper's plane had left.

It had been awful and Harper had felt utterly heartless.

But it had been the right thing to do because she and Yarran had been together so long—

too long. They'd been living on borrowed time. Eventually the relationship was bound to fail and Yarran would leave.

Like everyone else.

Harper knew Ali felt *acutely* every single sling and arrow her twin brother felt. She understood Yarran's pain was Ali's pain. That Yarran's heartbreak was just as visceral for his sister. She didn't blame Ali for being on Team Yarran. She didn't blame her for the ugly words. As someone who'd never really had a family, Harper knew better than any of their group how vital that was.

But it sure made her nervous tonight.

Especially with that hot kiss from Monday still playing over and over in her head. She didn't think Ali would still hate her for her desertion—they were all older and wiser and a lot of water had flowed under the bridge—but it didn't take a genius to figure out Ali would be super protective of Yarran. She wouldn't welcome any rekindling of their relationship. And she certainly wouldn't be happy about them seeing each other tomorrow night, no matter how pragmatic the reason.

And she sure as hell would not be happy about their make-out session at Yarran's.

'She won't bite, you know.'

'I know. But she has every right to be angry.'

'*What?*' Ivy squeaked indignantly as she rolled her eyes at Harper. 'It was *twelve* years ago, Harper. Yarran got past it. He married and had a kid, for crying out loud. *He's* fine. Well… I mean…apart from the whole widower thing but you know what I mean. And if *he* is, she should be, too!'

Harper shrugged. 'It's the twin thing, I guess. She was bound to feel his every emotion it more acutely given how in tune they are.'

'Even so. Time to forgive, don't you think?'

'Maybe.'

Harper loved Ivy's loyalty and practicality. As a former army brat, Ivy was used to rubbing along with people and her sunny personality had helped her fit in wherever she went. But Harper was a kid of the system and understood family dynamics in a way people with families never had to explore.

She could certainly see Ali's side. Harper's guilt was still acute at times why wouldn't Ali's rage be just as intense?

'She might just need some time to get used to having me around again, Ivy. I know you want us all to go back to being besties but let's cut her some slack, okay?'

Ivy pursed her lips. 'I guess. I just want it to be like it was.'

Harper smiled and nodded. 'Of course.' But,

unlike Ivy, she wasn't naïve enough to think that was possible. Harper had broken one of those unwritten rules—mess with a bestie's sibling at your own cost—and she knew it would take a while to win back Ali's trust.

Ivy paused outside a swish apartment block and Harper looked up. It was a groovy new low rise, lights shining from the apartments showcasing row upon row of balconies.

'C'mon.' She steered Harper in the direction of the doors. 'Let's get the hard part over and done with.'

Harper swallowed as her butterflies took flight.

The door opened abruptly to reveal a grinning Phoebe, her dark blonde hair as straight as always. Dr Phoebe Mason was Head of Neonatal Surgery and, like Ivy, was on the shorter, curvier side. 'Harper!' she exclaimed, practically vibrating with excitement.

'Phoebs!' she said as Phoebe yanked her close and hugged her.

Harper squeezed her eyes shut to stop the sudden spring of tears. She'd made a conscious decision to ease out of regular contact with Phoebe and Ivy over the years. They were all busy building careers that demanded insane hours so there hadn't been much time for more than a Happy Birthday/Merry Christmas message, anyway.

And setting the boundaries gave *her* the control.

'I missed you,' Phoebe whispered, emotion husking her voice. 'I'm so glad you're home.'

Home. The word had always felt foreign to Harper and yet being unconditionally accepted by these women had given her a sense of belonging her younger self had never imagined possible. She'd been a stranger, but they'd embraced her anyway—despite her inbuilt wariness—and held on tight.

Phoebe's hard hug went on and on and Harper, uncomfortable as ever with easy affection, laughed as she opened her eyes, about to protest being squeezed to death. Until her gaze met a dark brown one, eerily similar to Yarran's.

Alinta.

As fraternal twins Yarran and his sister didn't look particularly alike but their eyes? They were freakily identical.

The other woman's expression was cool and Harper's laughter faded as she and Ali shared a long, loaded look over Phoebe's shoulder. It had been a long time and yet it felt like no time at all as Harper stared at the woman who had dragged her into her circle at uni and then into her family home, involving her in the Edwardses' family life.

Introducing her to Yarran.

Ali had been thrilled at the developing relationship, encouraging it with outrageous enthusiasm and all the while hinting at her desire to be sisters one day.

Sisters. The magic word.

Harper had always longed for the unconditional love of a sibling. A real one, not another kid who just tolerated her presence in their house. And, in the end, she'd convinced herself that being with Yarran had been about that—finding a family—not *love.* And that wasn't fair to him. He'd deserved more than an ex-foster kid who didn't know *how* to be in a functioning, healthy relationship.

It had been one of the ways she'd justified walking away.

'Hi, Ali,' Harper murmured as she eased out of Phoebe's embrace.

Ali's nod was a little stiff but she managed a, 'Hi,' in return.

She wore a slim-fitting white vest top that practically glowed against her brown skin and showed off her toned arms. Like her mother, who had been an athletic champion in her day, Ali was long and lean, her brunette curls brushing the tops of her shoulders.

'It's nice to see you again,' Harper offered tentatively.

Harper didn't expect Ali to offer some kind of rote, polite reply—that wasn't Ali's way and she hadn't been seeking a compliment. It was just…the truth. It *was* nice to see her old friend again. Still, Harper was surprised to hear Ali say, 'Yeah. It's nice to see you, too.'

Their gazes held and while Harper saw an entire storm-tossed *ocean* of reserve in those freaky eyes, she also saw sincerity. The same kind of sincerity echoed in her voice.

And that would do for now.

'All righty, then,' Ivy said, grinning at both of them as she slid an arm around each one. 'Enough of the awkward stuff, I could murder a glass of wine.'

An hour later, Harper was feeling much more relaxed. They'd eaten amazing succulent Greek food, delivered from the local restaurant, out on the balcony then moved inside to sit on the floor around the coffee table eating freshly popped popcorn as they'd done when they'd been cramming for exams all those years ago. With no one on call, they'd even shared two bottles of red wine.

And they'd laughed. God, how they had *laughed*. So much and so hard as they'd caught up on years and years of stories Harper hadn't heard. Then it was her turn to share her own funny anecdotes for some laughter.

Sure, Ali's reserve was still in place, but she didn't make it awkward. In fact, Harper doubted Phoebe and Ivy were even aware of it. It was just that, like most ex-foster kids, Harper was intrinsically attuned to tension, her Spidey senses constantly alert to any frisson.

Which was fine. As Harper had told Ivy earlier, it was going to take some time.

But, she realised, sitting here with these women who had once meant so much to her, she *did* want to get the gang back together. Barring any unforeseen eventualities, Harper planned on being back in Sydney indefinitely and she'd missed female friendships, preferring to stay on the peripheries when she was in the UK.

But if she was truly coming home to finally put down some roots then that involved more than bricks and mortar and a regular pay cheque. It involved relationships. With *people*. And these three women were the best ones she knew.

She had to be *all in*.

'Any updates on Emma Wilson's condition, Phoebs?' Ali asked, switching the conversation back to present day.

As Head of Neonatal Surgery, Phoebe was part of the multi-disciplinary team consulting on the case. 'She's generally stable but quite oedematous and overloaded as all that fluid from her resus makes its way back into her system, which is putting a lot of extra work on her heart and lungs. The ICU team are having a tricky time trying to manage it all as well as juggle her sedation needs for her ventilation without potentially harming the babies.'

Ali nodded. 'Are they doing okay?'

'Surprisingly, yes. We're closely monitoring them and all seems to be in order but the fact is, while Emma is reasonably stable, she's still in a critical condition, so any number of things could suddenly happen necessitating the delivery of the twins and they're just far too little to be born right now.'

'How's her husband coping?' Ivy asked.

'He's trying to hold it all together,' Phoebe said. 'But it's hard, obviously. He's so focused on getting Emma through this and making sure we know *her* life is paramount, I think he's kind of disassociated from the babies. Which then makes him feel guilty because he knows Emma would want the opposite. He's seeing the ICU psychologist, but I think he feels stuck between a rock and a hard place.'

'God…' Harper was used to seeing difficult medical decisions play out in the ER so she knew how wrenching it could be for those grappling with them. 'The poor guy.'

Phoebe nodded. 'Yeah.'

'It must be hard for you, too, Phoebes,' Harper mused. 'Being the one having to prioritise the babies. Has that caused any issues?'

'Not issues, just trying to balance a lot of competing priorities. Like several calls a day from Lucas Matthews reminding me about the need for speed in the grafting process.'

Harper squinted as she thought back to Monday, trying to place the name. 'Lucas Matthews... He's Head of Reconstructive Surgery, right?'

'Yep,' Ivy confirmed, a flat edge to her voice and a curl to her lip. 'Couldn't have got a more perfect speciality for that pretty boy.'

Three sets of eyes flicked to Ivy, regarding her for a beat. 'What?' she demanded, scowling at each of them in equal measure.

Phoebe glanced at Ali then at Harper before looking back at Ivy. 'You have a problem with Lucas?'

'You mean apart from the fact he's arrogant and cocky, walking around the hospital in his Gucci suits with the most entitled swagger to ever swag?'

Phoebe did another glance around the circle. Ali lifted an eyebrow at Phoebe and pressed her lips together to suppress a smile. Phoebe followed suit. Harper's lips also twitched. It appeared Ivy might be protesting just a little too much.

'Well... I mean, he is very good-looking,' Ali murmured.

Ivy snorted. 'He *thinks* he's good-looking.'

Harper propped her chin on her hand. 'Yeah, I mean because hot, tall, super-competent guys in bespoke suits who probably drive a sports car and have that sexy greying-at-the-temples thing going on are generally considered unattractive.'

Phoebe and Ali both laughed out loud and Ali winked at Harper, causing her to catch her breath. It was such an inclusive gesture in this moment and warmth suffused her chest. She was home and although things hadn't got off to a great start with Yarran, she took heart that re-kindling her friendship with these women had.

Even Ali.

Phoebe pressed her lips together once more. 'Ivy, do you have a little crush?'

'What?' Ivy bugged her eyes at them. 'On that egotistical...? No way. I've learned my lesson with flashy, smooth-talking men.'

Ivy had filled Harper in on how badly burned she'd been by her cheating ex, Grant.

'Maybe,' Ali mused. 'But I think you're pro-testing a bit too much and you know the best way to get over one man, right?'

Phoebe's eyes sparkled as she waggled her eyebrows. 'Get under another one.'

'*Ew.*' Ivy's nose wrinkled. 'I'd rather perform an appendicectomy on myself without a general anaesthetic.'

More laughter as Ivy's cheeks grew pinker. 'Oh, honey,' Phoebe said, 'he's about as far from *ew* as possible. I mean, you don't like him? Sure. But, objectively, he is a very fine specimen of manhood.'

'You like him so much, *you* get under him.'

Casually, Phoebe plucked a kernel of popcorn out of the bowl and brought it to her mouth. 'Maybe I will,' she half whispered as she pushed the popcorn past her lips, watching Ivy as the other woman's mouth tightened.

Phoebe's grin grew at Ivy's obvious discombobulation. 'Ivy and Lucas sitting in a tree,' she sing-songed. 'K-I-S-S-I-N-G.'

Rolling her eyes, Ivy threw a piece of popcorn at Phoebe's forehead, which bounced right off. 'Oh, shut up,' she said, resigned to the teasing as they all dissolved into laughter.

'And what about you and love, Harper?' Phoebe asked.

Harper glanced at Ali as the question sat between them with the potential of an unexploded bomb. 'It's okay,' Ali assured her with a shrug. 'I assumed you'd moved on too.'

Ali couldn't have chosen her words better. The underlying message was that *Yarran* had moved on. That no matter how hurt he'd been he *had* moved on. And whether it was a deliberate message or not—Harper heard it loud and clear.

'So?' Ivy asked. '*Is* there anyone special waiting for you back in the UK?'

Harper shook her head. 'There's no one. I've been concentrating on my career.'

Ivy frowned. 'No one recently?'

Harper's gaze met Ali's. 'No one at all.'

'For *twelve* years?' Phoebe bugged her eyes. 'Are you telling me you haven't seen anyone in *twelve* years?'

Harper's eyes cut to Phoebe and she gave a half-laugh at her horrified expression. 'I've had a few brief, mutually beneficial, mutually pleasurable encounters. That's it.'

'Oh, thank God,' Ivy said, pressing a hand to her chest. 'You can't let that stuff build up. I don't believe in blocked chakras but hell… everyone needs to blow off a bit of steam.'

Harper had never been comfortable indulging in sexual gossip and she squirmed a little, very conscious of Ali sitting across the table. 'I hope you're taking your own advice, Ivy,' she deflected with a smile. 'I hear there's this guy who drives a sports car and wears Gucci who knows how to unblock a chakra or two.'

'Hmph.' Ivy went from relieved to irritated in a second, her brow wrinkling. 'I'm not letting *him* anywhere near my chakras.'

Ali, Phoebe and Harper laughed at the endearingly cranky expression on Ivy's face and the stubborn little set to her chin. Ivy picked up more popcorn and threw a kernel at each forehead, causing more laughter. And it was amidst all this friendly frivolity that Harper came to a decision. When the laughter started to die, she dropped her gaze to the popcorn and reached for a handful.

'I ran into Yarran.'

The words cut through any residual laughter like a lightsabre through a sponge cake. She hadn't been going to mention it, but it felt as if she and Ali were starting to build a rapport again and Harper knew that brother and sister talked all the time. If Yarran mentioned it and Harper didn't? It felt…deceptive.

As though she had something to hide.

And yes, okay, there was no need to reveal all the intimate details of their encounter, but not saying anything felt dishonest and Harper didn't want to start off on the wrong foot.

Phoebe and Ivy exchanged a look as Ali asked, 'When?'

'On Monday. At the hospital. With Emma.'

'Ah…' Ali nodded slowly. 'He didn't mention.'

Harper swallowed, dismay smothering her optimism as she watched the retreat in Ali's eyes as irrevocable as the outgoing tide. But the damage was done now so she might as well get it all out there. The PG bits, anyway. 'And later on, too.'

'Hey.' Ivy raised an eyebrow. 'You never mentioned you saw him twice?'

Ali's gaze cut to Ivy. 'You knew?'

Ivy opened her mouth to say something but Harper didn't give her a chance. 'We were leaving the hospital at the same time. He didn't have his car so I gave him a lift home.'

Ali blinked. 'I see.'

Nobody said anything for long silent moments. Harper could tell the other two women were dying to know the details but she also knew they wouldn't ask. Not right now.

'He's good now, Harper.'

Hot prickles stabbed at Harper's nape and she swallowed. 'I know.'

'He's *really* good now.'

'Nothing…' Harper let the word *happened* slip away unsaid. Now she'd decided to fess up there was no point compounding it with a lie. 'There's nothing between us.'

Which *wasn't* a lie. Sexual tension was inconvenient but it wasn't *feelings*.

'He wasn't for a long time,' Ali continued as if Harper hadn't spoken. 'And then there was Marnie and…' She drew in a shaky breath. 'He's been through a lot but he's finally *good*.'

Harper would have to have been deaf *not* to hear the message. Which was fine by her—she had no plans to rekindle their relationship. 'I *know*.'

Ali regarded her for long moments before giving a nod. 'Okay.'

'Okay.'

Ivy and Phoebe traded another look as the silence built again. 'Okay,' Ivy said, breaking the silence with a smile and a chirpy, 'Who wants coffee?'

Harper broke eye contact. 'Yes, please. I'll help.'

The tension eased as Harper stood and followed Ivy into the kitchen on very wobbly legs. Despite the loaded moments as she and Ali had faced each other across the coffee table, Harper was glad she'd spoken up. She wanted to re-enter this friendship circle, and this new part of her life, the way she meant to go on—openly and honestly.

Which would be a new concept given she'd never been fully open and honest with these women. Sure, her friends knew she'd had a rough childhood, that she'd been in the foster system, but she'd never gone into details. She knew that it was almost impossible for people who had grown up in *normal*—safe, functional, loving—families to truly understand the damage caused by the anxiety of impermanence.

But going forward, she'd like to be more open about the challenges of her upbringing.

So, that was the plan—a new kind of honesty. She just wasn't going to start with her and Yarran's passionate clinch. Because it had just been some weird slip of chemistry and nostalgia that had been bound to happen.

But *would not* happen again.

Sitting at the Opera Bar, with the iconic white sails of the Sydney Opera House rising majestically before him and the lit-up façade of the Harbour Bridge behind, Yarran checked his watch for the third time. Harper was fifteen minutes late.

Now there was something he *hadn't* missed.

Being involved with a doctor meant a lot of running late for dates—not that this was a date—and sometimes even last-minute cancellations. Because something had come up at the hospital or her pager had gone off a few minutes before she was due to finish or a resus case had just come through the doors.

And he was fine with all that. He got it. He

was an emergency worker too. You couldn't put down a hose or stop in the middle of CPR because your shift had officially ended. It was just that, tonight, her lateness was giving him a lot of time to think.

Too much time to think.

About that kiss. About how much he *shouldn't* be thinking about that kiss. About the attraction sizzling between them more electric than ever. About how twelve years could pass and yet his pulse still skittered when he saw her that first time as if they'd never been apart.

He'd convinced himself it had been like muscle memory for him. He'd once loved Harper deeply and their chemistry had been insane. You couldn't just switch that kind of thing off—it needed to burn out. And it had still been blazing when she'd run away, so their heated making out had been inevitable in a lot of ways.

But that was *done* now. Out of the system. And after their talk tonight, hopefully a few other demons would be put to rest so they could get on with being friends. Something they perhaps should have stayed all those years ago—for everyone's sake.

'Oh, God, Yarran… I'm so sorry.'

Yarran dragged his gaze off the city skyline and the reflection of the lights on the black surface of the harbour to find Harper hurrying towards him looking harried, her loose red hair flying around her head. A sheer, silky wrap slipped down her arms as the satiny skirt of her shamrock-green dress streamed behind her, the fabric outlining the shape of her thighs.

He half stood but she waved him down as she pulled out her chair and sat opposite.

'Traffic has got so much worse, hasn't it? The Uber driver got me as close as he could.'

'Yeah, a lot has changed in twelve years.'

Maybe if he said it out loud, he'd remember because, looking at her all fresh and lovely and so damn close he could reach out and touch, nothing felt *done* about them.

'This hasn't though,' she said as she took a moment to look around. *'Wow.'* She shook her head. 'It's a pretty spectacular sight.'

It *was* spectacular, sitting here at a waterside table on the lower concourse of Bennelong Point, the harbour lapping below the solid fluted cement railings. It was still warm out for a May evening and people were taking full advantage of the weather while it lasted.

Light glimmered all around them from the neon of the skyline to the warm glow of streetlights on the upper concourse, to the way the Opera House was lit both inside and out. White lights on the sails emphasised their curves and made them appear almost luminescent while the internal yellow glow shone out through the glass curtain walls.

Everything sparkled and he was glad he'd thought to book here just to see the lights shimmering in her clear lip gloss.

'It is,' he said. And so was she.

A waiter approached and asked Harper if she wanted a drink. She cast a quick eye at Yarran's frosty beer glass before ordering. 'A Prosecco, please.'

'You want something to eat?' Yarran asked as the waiter departed. He handed over a menu, which she declined.

'No, thanks. I'm fine for now.'

She folded her arms on the table in front of her and looked around her again, checking out the people this time. 'Gosh, it's busy,' she murmured.

Yarran nodded, non-committal, too busy looking at her to pay heed to anyone else. He couldn't drag his eyes off her. Off the way her hair brushed her shoulders, the way the fabric of her dress sat against the slope of her breasts.

The shine of that lip gloss.

And he couldn't think of a single thing to say because all he could think about was the kiss. *He couldn't stop thinking about the kiss*. He was supposed to be here clearing the air and yet he couldn't get the smell or the taste of her out of his head. He couldn't *not* remember the way she had shifted in his arms, the way she'd moaned.

He hadn't looked at or thought about another woman since Marnie's death and here he was—sitting opposite his first love, with every brain cell he owned on the fritz.

But then she looked at him and said, 'Who's looking after Jarrah tonight?' and it was like a defib to the electrical dysfunction storming his body.

Jarrah. His son, his heart, his life. His reason to get up in the morning.

Finding and losing love twice had been a painful way for Yarran to learn he couldn't count on romantic love. But the love for his child? *That* was everything. And he thanked the universe Harper had given him something else to think about.

'He's at Mum and Dad's.'

'And did you...' she hesitated '...tell your mum where you were going or who you were meeting?'

'No.'

'She didn't ask?'

Yarran chuckled. 'Are you kidding? Mum was so pleased I was actually going out somewhere socially she didn't dare question it in case I changed my mind.'

Harper laughed. 'Not much of a carouser these days?'

'Ah…no.'

He had been for sure, back in the day. *Before she'd walked out of his life.* But he wasn't going to point that out. Not when her voice was light and her hazel eyes were sparkling. He didn't want to spoil the moment.

'I guess having a four-year-old is not conducive to carousing?'

'No.' He laughed. 'Definitely not.'

'Tell me about him,' she requested. 'Jarrah. If you don't mind?'

Yarran regarded her, ignoring the warmth in his belly. She was curious—it was only natural. And it was what people did, when you had kids—they asked after them. It was polite conversation. 'I don't mind.'

'Do you have pictures?'

'Duh.' He rolled his eyes as he pulled out his phone.

For the next half an hour he talked about his son—a topic on which Yarran could chat for *hours*. He talked about how he'd been a colicky baby and how he'd walked early and the trials and tribulations of getting him to eat vegetables when he'd happily survive on bananas and fairy bread. He talked about how he suddenly needed a night light because he was going through an afraid-of-the-dark phase and how he loved mucking around in the garden with Yarran and adored flowers and how he called his aunt Alinta *Li-Li*, and how he was looking forward to his fourth birthday party in a few weeks.

Four years old. God…where had that time gone?

He didn't mention Marnie. Or that Jarrah had no memory of his mother. Or that for months after the car accident, Yarran had *let* Jarrah eat nothing but bananas and fairy bread because at least it was calories and just surviving the day had been hard enough without throwing in a tantrum or two.

Whether that was because it felt strange mentioning one woman he'd loved to the woman he'd loved *first*, or whether he just didn't want to go down that emotional rabbit hole on a night they were supposed to be talking about *them*, he wasn't sure. And maybe she sensed that because she didn't ask either.

She shook her head as she gazed down at a picture of Jarrah raking a garden bed with his grandfather. 'Man…he looks like your dad.'

Yarran laughed. 'Yep.' It was odd because he and Ali, despite their non-identical appearance, both looked more like their mother, and like their mother's aunties and uncles, who still lived on Gundungurra and Darug country near the Blue Mountains just outside Sydney.

'How are they?' she asked, handing back his phone. 'Your parents? All those siblings of yours?'

'They're great.'

Yarran smiled, conscious, as always, of that note of envy in her voice. Harper had adored his big, loud, messy family but he'd known, without her having to say it, they were a double-edged sword. The Edwards mob made Harper acutely aware of her *lack* of family.

'Mum's now an indigenous liaison for Olympic athletes and Dad's resisting retiring from the ambulance service but he does some lecturing for the intensive care paramedic course at the uni a couple of days a week, so he has taken a step back from active service.'

Yarran was pretty sure they'd have to push Coen Edwards out on one of those flashy stretchers.

'Kirra, Lucca and Marli all have kids. In fact, Marli is pregnant with number three. There're ten cousins altogether and I'm their favourite uncle.'

Harper laughed as she reached for her Prosecco. 'You were always king of the kids.'

Something thunked hard deep inside Yarran's chest. It was true—kids had always gravitated towards him. It was the fire-truck thing mostly, but he'd always been up for pushing a swing or a piggyback ride.

He wanted to ask her about children but she'd been adamantly opposed to having any during their time together. And, knowing a bit about her background, Yarran had never really pushed. Nor was he going to, tonight. She was forty years old; he figured if she was going to change her mind, she probably would have by now.

The rosemary fries and second beer he ordered arrived and they paused their conversation momentarily. Yarran watched Harper as she turned her head to take in the harbour view, a light breeze ruffling her hair, those familiar flyaway wisps at her temples as fascinating as always.

The waiter departed and Yarran pushed the bowl of chips into the middle of the table. 'Tell me about your time in the UK,' he said as he took one.

'What?' She grinned. '*All* of it?'

Yarran's breath stilled in his lungs. When she smiled like that, so candid and unguarded, it lit up her whole face and he'd loved this side of Harper. It had taken him so long to work through her defences, to be trusted enough. But breaking through had been utterly rewarding— despite her frequent relapses.

Being with Harper had sometimes felt as if he were constantly reinventing the wheel but she'd been worth it. And that was what people did for those they loved.

It was what he did, anyway.

'Fine,' he said, recovering his senses and his breath. 'Give me the CliffsNotes.'

By the time she'd given him the rundown, they'd laughed a lot more and they'd been at the bar for an hour. Two drinks each had been consumed and Harper was relaxed and happy and maybe it wasn't the best time but the question he'd been swallowing down came to the fore and he couldn't stop it any longer.

'Why'd you come back, Harper?'

Slowly her smiled faded, her gaze holding his for what felt like an eternity. She tucked her hair over an ear, exposing one of her gold hoop ear-rings, which had been playing peek-a-boo all night. Her fingers absently toyed with the hoop as she parted her lips to speak.

Nothing came out as she continued to maintain their eye-lock and Yarran's ribcage rocked with the hard thud of his heart as he waited. For one crazy beat he thought she was going to say *because of you*. I came back *because of you*. But then she closed her mouth and her gaze shifted over his shoulder and he castigated himself for such fanciful thinking.

As if he were in a position—or stupid enough—to risk love again with Harper.

Her eyes flicked back to his face and Yarran knew, whatever she'd been going to say—that moment had passed. 'I was…headhunted. And…' she shrugged '…the job was great, just what I was looking for—the next step in my career. The perfect step, actually.'

He nodded slowly. Harper's career focus had always been laser-like. And he'd loved that about her. She'd grown up with *nothing*, and yet she'd made it into med school and she'd been determined not to squander the opportunity. 'It's a prestigious role. Ali said there were several high-level candidates.'

'There were. I'm very fortunate.'

'No.' If there was one thing he knew about Harper Jones, it was how hard she worked. And she was a brilliant doctor. They didn't give out prestigious head of department jobs to people who weren't the top in their field. '*You're* good.'

She shrugged and said, 'That too,' then laughed.

Yarran joined her. He'd always found her unshakable confidence in her medical skill a turn-on. It had been such a stark contrast to her ingrained insecurities. So when it flashed out like this, like a beacon from a lighthouse, it hit him with a hot jab to his groin.

'And you,' she said, a smile still hovering on her mouth. 'Ivy tells me you're a captain now. You must be close to making chief. That's what you wanted, right?'

'Mmm.' Yarran leaned forward, propping his elbow on the table and his chin on his palm. 'Not any more. Or at least not now, anyway. It's a lot of extra work and while Jarrah's so young... I mean, Mum and Dad are great, but they have a life too and... I don't know. I guess my priorities changed after...'

His words drifted away and she just nodded, clearly not requiring him to clarify. 'And besides,' he said with a smile, shaking himself out of the drag of old memories, 'who wants to be chained to a desk when I can be facing down a roaring fire?'

A half-laugh slipped between her parted lips as she shook her head. 'As long as I live, I will never get the attraction to something so dangerous and, well...*hot*.'

Yarran grinned. 'We're a special breed.'

She laughed again. 'You are.'

The waiter approached and asked if they'd like another drink and Harper shook her head. 'No, thank you.' She glanced at him. 'I should go. I told Ivy I'd only be a couple hours.'

'Of course.' Given the easy mood between them and the low buzz of attraction fizzing thorough his veins, it was probably wise to quit while they were ahead. They hadn't really talked about their issues, but they had proven they could be in each other's company and not argue or jump each other.

'Can I give you a lift?'

For a moment she looked startled at his offer before she shook her head. 'Oh, no, you're in the opposite direction, it's fine.' Grabbing her bag, she hauled out her phone. 'I'll just order an Uber.'

Yarran's eyes roved over her profile, the warm hue from the candle picking out gold highlights in her hair. 'I have my car, Harper. And it'll give us the chance to talk a bit more. Please, let me return the favour.'

She glanced up from her phone, indecision writ large across her features as she caught her bottom lip between her teeth. Maybe she was trying to duck the conversation they'd avoided so succinctly or maybe she was remembering what had happened last time they'd shared a car. He gave a self-deprecating smile. 'I won't come up.'

Harper gave a rueful smile in return. 'Okay.' She put her phone in the bag and pulled her gauzy wrap up over her shoulders. 'Thanks.'

CHAPTER FOUR

WITHIN FIFTEEN MINUTES of leaving the restaurant, Yarran was pulling out into traffic. They hadn't talked very much on the short walk to the car park. There'd been so much going on around them with the city sights and the throngs of people out enjoying the delights of Darling Harbour, conversation hadn't been necessary. But, as he drove and she sat quietly in the passenger seat looking out of the window, the silence grew more and more loaded.

Yarran was trying to parse which words to use to break it, when Harper got in first.

'I didn't just come back for the job,' Harper said, her eyes still trained on the view outside her window. 'I've missed waking up to kookaburras in the morning and Christmases on the beach and looking up and seeing the southern cross. Seeing stars full stop.' She shook her head slowly as she stared outward. 'Not a lot of stars in London.'

'No.' Yarran had been to London twice. Once for a high-school trip when he was fifteen. The other with Marnie for the first wedding anniversary. It had been weird knowing Harper was in the same city.

'I missed my friends,' she continued. 'I missed…'

His throat grew thick as he pulled up at a red light, his fingers tightening around the wheel. Was she going to say she'd missed *him*?

Did he want her to?

'I missed home. I didn't know—with all the crap in my childhood—that I was capable of that. Which made it easy and almost…freeing when I left here but…despite everything, I realise I did.' She rolled her head along the backrest until she was facing him. 'You know?'

'Uh-huh.'

He did know. The blood of his indigenous ancestors, his mother's stories, the presence of mob in his life, had imbued him with a keen connection to country and that ancient pull of home had always grounded him. But for someone who'd only known dislocation, who had felt rootless all her life? He supposed that *would* make leaving easy.

'Twelve years is a long time to be away from home,' he murmured.

She gave a small smile. 'Yeah.' Then turned back to the view.

The light turned green and Yarran accelerated away, wondering if maybe their past was better left in the past. Tonight had proven they could be around each other and get on in polite company—maybe that was enough.

'I'm sorry about the way it ended.'

Yarran's fingers tightened around the steering wheel. 'It's fine, don't worry about it.'

'No, it's not.' She half turned in her seat to face him. 'It's why we're here, tonight, isn't it? So let's talk about it.'

He flicked a glance at her before returning his attention to the road. Her brow was furrowed and her mouth was set in a stubborn little line he knew too well, the green of her dress in the darkened confines of the cab turned up the glitter in her hazel eyes. At the start of the night, *this* had been his agenda but, surprisingly now, he was willing to let it go.

What would be the point in dissecting everything from over a decade ago? Would hearing her say she'd missed him, that she'd come back for him, make a difference? When they were ancient history? When they were nothing more—could be nothing more—than two missed connections.

'My life was going so well and…that never

worked out for me in the past. Something was always around the corner, ready to take it all away. So... I learned to mistrust that feeling and to try and get out ahead of whatever was around the corner.'

Yarran had always suspected this about her, he just wished she could have spoken to him about it when they were together. Wished he'd prodded more. 'Did you think I'd stop loving you?'

'Like everybody else in my life?' She turned back to the window but not before he saw the shimmer of tears. 'Yes.'

'I wouldn't have.' He knew that as sure as he knew up was up and down was down.

'Life taught me to never get comfortable staying in one place too long and I'd well and truly pushed the boundaries with you because I loved you and I wanted normal so bad, but normal never lasted very long for me and people around us were talking marriage and kids and I started to feel...hemmed in. It made me nervous and... itchy. Like ants marching under my skin. And the job was there and it seemed like a lifeline but... I didn't know you were going to propose that night, Yarran.'

'I know.'

'And when you did, all I could see was *disas-*

ter, a slow-moving car crash from which I might never recover. So, I panicked.'

'Yeah.'

She looked over at him. 'I truly never meant to hurt you, but I know I did and I am really, really sorry.'

Yarran nodded. She hadn't apologised that night. Hell, she hadn't even apologised when she'd visited before she left in her attempt to *set things right*. She'd been brash and confrontational, talking about it being *her* life, and how *she* got to decide what she did with it. Obviously, she hadn't ever had anyone apologise unequivocally to her in her life and just hadn't known *how*.

But she clearly needed to now and do it properly so she'd obviously come a long way during her years overseas. 'Thank you,' he said, smiling at her as he decelerated to turn into the street where Ivy's apartment was situated.

He was surprised at how much hearing her finally say the *s* word had actually helped and wondered, as he navigated the right turn, if saying it had also helped her. Wondered, too—not for the first time—if maybe she would benefit from another kind of help. Like talking to a professional about her childhood traumas.

Yarran had skirted the issue when they'd been together, but Harper had always clammed up at the merest suggestion and, well…basically he'd been too much of a coward to persist. He'd been too scared, or maybe just too selfish, to jeopardise what they had.

Maybe that was forgivable in his early twenties but at forty? With the benefit of hindsight and carrying the weight of his own trauma on his shoulders?

'Do you think it might be possible to be friends?' she asked. 'I'm loving being back with Ivy and Phoebe and Ali but…your sister is obviously wary and I'm not blaming her,' she hastened to add. 'She's pissed at me for hurting you and I get that. But maybe if you and I were friends she'd see that if *we're* happy to move on from the past then maybe she could, too? I know it's a lot to ask and maybe you need some more time to—'

'No,' Yarran interrupted. 'I don't. I would very much like to be your friend, Harper Jones.' It'd have to be easier than this strange kind of limbo they were in now.

But maybe he should start as he meant to go on? That was what *friends* were for, right?

Pulling into the loading zone in front of Ivy's apartment, he switched the engine off and turned in his seat slightly to face her. The street outside was deserted and not well lit, the dashboard glow the only light inside the car.

'Please don't take this the wrong way,' he said, his voice low but resonant in the fat bubble of silence between them. 'But…have you ever thought about seeing a therapist?'

She didn't say anything for a long time, her gaze drifting to the windscreen. Twenty-year-old Yarran would have backpedalled about now but silences weren't as scary at forty.

'Just…you know.' He smiled at her profile. 'One friend to another.'

She laughed then, her gaze cutting back to him. 'Yes.' She sighed. 'Then I usually do something to distract myself until the thought goes away.'

Yarran grinned. 'Very mature.'

She arched an eyebrow. 'Right?'

They grinned at each other but it was brief as they both sobered. 'Honestly, Harper, isn't it exhausting carrying around all your stuff? Feeling *hemmed in*, feeling like something's always just around the corner waiting to turn your life upside down?'

'Yeah.' She nodded slowly. 'Very.'

His words weren't said with any kind of pity, but her response sounded so forlorn something broke a little inside Yarran and he desperately wanted to pull her in for a hug. Instead he said, 'I saw a therapist for a while. After…' He swallowed. It wasn't easy to talk to Harper about Marnie. 'After my wife died. It helped.'

'I know.' Her glance returned to the windscreen. 'I do know and it's on my to-do list.' She gave a half-laugh. 'See shrink is right after rekindle old friendships, move into new apartment and become the best damn director of ER to have ever existed.'

She glanced back at him and smiled, which Yarran returned. He knew she was joking, maybe seeking some levity in a heavy moment, but he sincerely hoped she did follow through. He didn't know half the stuff she'd been through, and he had no medical training, but he knew enough about grief and loss to know sometimes it was just too heavy to deal with alone.

'Thank you,' she said, her voice soft as she slid her hand onto his forearm and gave it a squeeze. 'I'm glad we did this.'

There was nothing sexual about the touch. It was impersonal. One of those gestures between *friends* but while Yarran's head was on board with the *friend* thing, his body was clearly not. He was so conscious of her in this moment— aware of her nearness, of their aloneness, of the dark enclosed confines—every hair on his body prickled with awareness.

He could smell her perfume—something fresh and zesty—and wondered if she still dabbed it behind her knees. His pulse surged in his belly and through his groin, his breath suddenly hot as lava in his lungs.

Yarran cleared his throat. 'Me too.' And he *was*. Or he would be. Once she was out of his car and the temptation had passed.

She smiled and leaned in, her hand still on his forearm, for what he assumed was a friendly peck and he shut his eyes as her lips touched down on a point midway between his cheekbone and his mouth. It was nothing more than a brush of her lips but it might as well have been a full-on pash as sensation rushed *everywhere*.

Hell, he could barely breathe for the calamity of it.

And that was when he became aware she wasn't shifting away. Her lips had stayed well past what could be considered chaste and had moved to lingering. It was certainly no peck. In fact, he was damn sure it had turned into a *nuzzle* as her fingers curled into the flesh of his forearm and a warm sigh brushed his skin.

'Harper,' he whispered, angling his head a little to facilitate her nuzzling even as the backbeat in his brain was blaring, *Friends, friends, friends.*

But then a small, almost *feral* kind of noise slipped from the back of her throat blaring *want* and *lust* and *need*, spiking Yarran's pulse and clutching at his groin, and whatever tenuous hold he had over his libido snapped clean in two.

'God... *Harper*...' He turned his face, to nuzzle her. Her cheek, her temple, her ear. His senses filled with the aroma of her shampoo and something far...earthier. Her eyes were fever bright as his hands cupped her face. 'Why can't I stop wanting you?' he whispered as he took her mouth with his.

Her answer, if there was one, was lost to a rush of heat obliterating sense and noise and freaking *time*. Yarran was aware of nothing outside the press of their lips, the hammer of his heart, the harsh suck of his breath competing with the harsh suck of hers. Not until her hand moved, anyway, sliding up his chest, her fingers hooking into the fabric of his shirt as she leaned fully into the kiss.

He leaned in too, the centre console the only thing stopping them from full upper-body contact, but that didn't stop his hand from travelling down her arm and onto her hip because he *had* to touch her—he *needed* to touch her. She tasted of Prosecco and smelled like a shot of Limoncello, and Yarran wanted to gulp her down more than he wanted his next breath as his fingers dug in, urging her closer. His tongue tangled with hers and she whimpered in a way so *unholy* it was like a punch of hot lead to his groin.

Christ, he *wanted* her. Right here, right now. In his car. In the front of her apartment.

A sudden bang from outside eviscerated that thought as Harper tore away from him, sucking in air, blinking dazedly, as if she hadn't quite been in her body.

He knew how she felt.

It took Yarran several seconds to compute the scene before him. One guy thumping on the bonnet of the car like a drum, two of his friends laughing and hollering behind as they pointed at the car. None of them appeared to be able to stand very steadily.

'*Oi!* You two,' drummer boy said. 'Get a room!' He gave one last thump and they all weaved away, laughing too loud, clearly thinking themselves hilarious.

Yarran glanced at Harper, who was looking at him with equal discombobulation. Silence filled the space between them as Yarran tried to pull something coherent together in his muddled brain. To make sense of what had just happened—the act, not the interruption.

Because it sure as hell didn't make any sense to him. The first time maybe, at his house, he could understand. But this time? How had they gone from 'let's be friends' to necking like teenagers in a matter of minutes?

'Harper... I—'

'No.' She shook her head. 'It's okay.' She patted his chest absently before withdrawing her hand. 'We'll get better at the friends thing.'

He huffed out a husky laugh. 'Really?'

She stared at him, her gaze brushing over his mouth and for a moment Yarran thought she might actually come back in for more, but then she gave her head a shake. 'I've got to go.'

'Okay.'

'We *will* get better,' she said before opening her door and slipping away.

Yarran sincerely hoped so. They could hardly get worse.

'Okay, ready?' Harper asked the three nurses standing around the stretcher bed where an unwell, grizzly toddler—Remi—was looking up at them, eyes bright with fever and round with terror. His tearful mother was up near the head of the bed, stroking his hair and dropping tiny kisses on his forehead as she whispered soothing words. She'd been up for three nights in a row with her sick child and was exhausted both physically and emotionally.

It wasn't often the head of the department was called on to put in an IV, but children were often tricky to cannulate—dehydrated ones even more so. Two attempts had already been made by more junior doctors leading to an overwrought child and an even more stressed mama. But Remi needed fluids so the big boss—who'd been on her way out of the door—had been put on the job.

Harper had done a year at Great Ormond Street in London, during which time she'd inserted hundreds of cannulas into children in varying places—hands, arms, feet and even scalps. And she knew she could get this one into a vein in Remi's foot, as long as he was still.

Sure, the area had been numbed and Remi wouldn't feel the needle going in but it was psychological now. The child was already deeply mistrustful of them, breathing choppily as he looked at the faces above him, clearly contemplating leaping up and running away.

Hence the *muscle*.

'Okay, little dude.' She smiled at Remi, whose chin started to wobble as she tightened the tourniquet sitting just above his ankle. 'Mummy's going to count to twenty and then we'll be done, okay?'

She crossed her fingers behind her back, hoping like hell it was so. She didn't, necessarily, have a problem stretching the truth a little if it helped allay a child's—and their parent's—fear. But it suddenly struck her that Remi was the same age as Jarrah and somehow it just seemed more...personal.

He started to cry as soon as the nurses took their positions. The one closest to Harper—Darren, an Englishman who'd been in Australia for ten years—held the foot around the ankle and at the toes, angling it to best expose the vein. The second leaned in over Remi's knees and legs while the third did the same for his torso. They weren't lying across him as of yet but they were primed to do so should Remi start to buck and squirm.

With the area already cleaned, Harper picked up the cannula off the trolley by her side and lined it up where it looked like the best insertion point a few millimetres from the skin. 'Okay, Mummy, let's do it.'

The mother started to count haltingly, her voice thick with emotion, which was Remi's cue to cry then wriggle. The nurses at his legs and torso used their weight to gently restrict his movement and Darren held the ankle a little firmer as the needle tip touched down.

'Good boy, Remi,' Darren said in his booming Geordie accent. 'You're doing well, mate. As soon as we're done here, I'm going to make you a glove animal.'

Far from placated, Remi cried louder—more from the restraint, Harper suspected, than the prick—and wriggled harder in their grasp. Thankfully he was sufficiently confined for

Harper to do her job. Blocking out the frantic little boy's cries and the choked sobs of his mother, Harper was able, after minimal manoeuvring, to slide the cannula into the vein.

'Done,' she announced triumphantly, raising her voice to be heard over the crying as she unclipped the tourniquet. 'Just gotta tape it now and it's all over.'

One-handed, she grabbed the short extension tubing already primed with a saline syringe attached, then she removed the inner needle to leave the plastic cannula straw in situ. A bleb of blood swelled at the cannula hub but didn't spill due to the pressure she was applying over the cannula tip on the outside. Quickly, she twisted the extension tube in place and flushed the line.

The saline flowed in smoothly and she nodded with satisfaction. Bridie, the nurse across Remi's torso, eased off to help Harper tape the cannula in place and within two minutes they had it secured, the foot had been boarded and wrapped in a bandage and Remi was sitting cuddled up in his mother's arms.

A rush of something utterly foreign flushed through Harper's chest at the sight. She'd never known the mother-child bond but, watching Remi and his mum, she was struck by how much it resonated.

What the hell?

Confused, she turned to Darren, who was currently blowing air into a glove as if it were a balloon, puffing up the fingers like udders.

'I'll write up some fluid orders,' she said, and then she fled the cubicle.

In fact, after she'd written the orders, she fled all the way to the rooftop garden. Her shift was over—although she was on call tonight—and she was waiting to hear from Ivy about whether she wanted a lift home. And up here was as good as any place to wait—quiet and peaceful, the gardens beautiful, the view amazing and the evening lovely. The sky was a palate of pinks and mauves with the evening star now shining bright.

She could breathe up here. She could think. It was Wednesday and she hadn't had time to think much about Saturday night. The ER had been exceptionally busy, which had given her no time to mull over the *friendship* between her and Yarran.

Not coherently, anyway. With all that analytical thinking she supposedly possessed.

The night-time thinking didn't count. It wasn't analytical. It was hot and hazy and restless, those kisses playing on repeat as she tried to wrangle her body from arousal to practicality. They'd agreed to be friends so fantasising about his kisses was pointless. And now a mother and child making her feel restless but in a different way—what was that about?

Coming home, it seemed, was rousing a whole bunch of feelings both familiar and foreign and, although she didn't regret it, she hadn't expected to feel so whammed. It had been *twelve* years and yet, when Yarran had asked her on Saturday night why she'd come back, for one crazy moment she almost said *because of you*.

Which was madness.

Yarran hadn't entered the equation at all. She'd known she'd be in his sphere, of course, but she'd figured they'd moved on and were both adults. Yet it had been right there, on the tip of her tongue. She'd almost said it.

Because of you. For no earthly reason…

The door opened and Harper glanced over her shoulder to see Aaron Wilson stepping into the garden. Their eyes met and she saw the moment he recognised who she was. 'Hey,' he said as he ambled in her direction, crossing to where she stood at the railing.

'Hey,' she replied politely.

'You're the doctor, from the ER, right?'

'Yeah.' Harper smiled sympathetically. He was a good-looking guy—she was sure the TV cameras ate him up—his indigenous heritage affording him the noble bone structure and poise of his ancestors. And yet, right now he looked a worrying combination of haggard and wired. As if he was surviving on very little sleep and a lot of bad hospital coffee.

'Harper,' she said and held out her hand.

They shook then Aaron leaned his elbows on the railing and stared out over the city lights, a slow steady breath leaving his lungs, as if he'd been holding it in for a while.

'You hiding from them?' she asked, tipping her chin at the reporters down below still hanging around the entrance. Their number had decreased over the last week but there were still a few die-hards hanging on.

He stared down at them and muttered, 'Bloody vultures.'

Neither of them said anything for long silent moments before Harper broke the peace. 'How are they going? Emma and the babies?'

'Stable, they say. But...' He didn't turn from the view, just stared straight ahead.

Harper nodded. She knew *stable* still looked pretty dire to the lay person. 'Yeah.'

'Plastics wants to start Emma's grafting so they're just trying to work out the best approach for her and the twins.'

'There's a lot to consider.' It *wasn't* a straightforward burns case after all.

'Too much. When I think of everything that's ahead of us…'

'It's a lot,' Harper agreed. 'Just gotta take it one day at a time.'

'So they keep saying.' He gave a harsh humourless laugh.

'Please know you couldn't have a better team looking after them. Lucas and Ivy and Alinta and Phoebe—they're the best.'

He nodded. 'Yeah, I do know, I'm very happy with what they're doing for Emma and the babies, it's just…' He stared out at the light again. 'You know, you're going along and you think life is good, and you have it all, and then *bam*! It can just be gone in a flash. And you realise none of it means anything if the people you love are hurting or in trouble.'

Harper had always felt pretty much alone but she knew what it felt like to be blindsided by the unexpected. She'd spent a lifetime in flight mode trying to keep one step ahead of the unexpected, after all. 'Yeah, things like that make you reassess your priorities.'

Her phone rang and she pulled it out of her scrub pocket. 'Sorry, I have to take this.'

He nodded. 'Of course.'

'I'll see you around.'

'Yeah.'

Harper answered as she crossed the roof to the door. 'Hey, Ivy.'

'Sorry, I just got a ward call to a hot appendix. I'm taking it straight to Theatre. I'll see you in a couple of hours.'

'No worries.' That was the doctor life, after all.

Ivy hung up as Harper opened the door and stepped inside. Forgoing the lift, she crossed to the fire escape and took the stairs. Her phone vibrated in her hand and she almost stumbled at the name on the screen. A text from Yarran.

I have something of yours. Ring me when you're free.

If he only knew he had more of her than was good for her sanity. But she smiled at the screen and before she could second-guess herself, she tapped on the message and called him as she made her way down the fire escape.

'That was quick.'

His voice was warm as honey in her ear and she almost stumbled again. She gave up trying to multitask and stopped, leaning her butt against the cold wall of the stairwell.

'Phone was in my hand.' Harper stared at her shoes. 'You have something of mine?'

'I do. It's green and silky.'

Harper could hear the amusement in his voice and her belly clenched as she thought back to Saturday night. The wrap. She must have left it in his car. 'Oh, I didn't even know it was missing.' She *had* been kind of bamboozled when she'd exited his car.

'I think it must have slipped off your arms when…'

Her breath caught as his voice trailed off. *When they'd been necking like teenagers?* And sprung like teenagers, too.

'Anyway,' he continued, 'I was looking for a toy car of Jarrah's under the seat when I came across it. It must have slid down between the seat and the centre console.'

Very probably. Considering how her hands had been all over him. Harper cleared her throat. 'Okay, thanks. Where is it now?'

'It's still in the car. I can drop it in to the hospital or to Ivy's? Or did you want to come and pick it up?'

No. God, *no*. The last thing she needed was for Ali to see him dropping off her wrap. Or for Ivy to be home when he called. And going to his place? Yeah, not after last time. She was all for getting their friendship on track but it was probably best in the company of others.

Maybe they could meet out somewhere? With lots of people. Then go their separate ways. She pulled her bottom lip between her teeth. 'Where are you now?'

'I'm at work. Second of three nights.'

'Excellent.' Perfect, actually. Dropping by the firehouse would be public and, given he was at work, she wouldn't be able to linger. 'Can I drop by now and pick it up?'

'Works for me.'

'All right. See you soon.'

Harper pulled up outside Yarran's fire house forty minutes later after driving through a KFC window and grabbing two buckets of fried chicken and a dozen boxes of chips. She knew, both from her prior association with Yarran and through her work in the ER, how hard firefighters worked, the risks they took with their lives.

And how much they liked to eat.

She wasn't a baker or a Michelin-starred chef but she did have a credit card and she wasn't afraid to use it to show her appreciation for these guys and what they did. Plus, as a fellow shift worker she knew how much the night shift sucked.

Also, she was starving. One serving of chips had already made its way into her stomach.

Hiding the bag of food behind her back, Harper rang the night bell at the front door. The engine-bay doors were all shut but light shone through the narrow windows situated above the doors and through the windows of the adjoining building, which was where the bell was located and where, she assumed, the fire crews did their thing when not on truck.

Harper was surprised when a blond Adonis in his mid-twenties answered and not Yarran. 'Hey…' he said, laying a *How you doin'?* smile on her as he leaned into the door frame.

'Oh. Hi… I'm looking for Yarran Edwards?'

He clutched his chest in a dramatic fashion and grinned. 'That old guy? Could I interest you in someone a little younger? Better moves. More stamina?'

Harper laughed at the flirting—it was impossible not to. 'It's nothing like that,' she assured him. 'We're just friends. I'm just here to pick up something. And also, I bought this.'

She produced the bag of fast food, which had the desired effect. 'Where can I get a friend like you?' He grabbed the bag. 'Brock,' he said, holding out his hand.

She shook. 'Harper.'

Brock gestured her in with a flurry of his hand. 'Entray vooze.'

She laughed at his butchery of the French language as she stepped into a foyer area with several offices and a staircase rising in front of her.

'He's up there talking on the phone to the big boss. C'mon, I'll show you.'

Harper followed him up the stairs, which was no hardship—Brock had a fine-looking butt. 'Heads up,' he announced, raising his voice a little, as he climbed. 'We got female company so everyone put their clothes on.' Brock reached the top and turned left. 'Also.' He lifted the bag in the air. 'We got chicken.'

There was whooping and hollering as Harper reached the top and also turned left to find a large open room with a huge-screen TV on one wall and a fully kitted-out kitchen on the opposite one with a long dining table off to one side. Several couches were scattered around and, in the middle, six guys sat around a coffee table playing cards.

Far from undressed, they were all in their fire-issue cargo pants and navy T-shirts. Okay, they weren't all as cockily good-looking or young as Brock—there was a range of ages and sizes—but they were all big and solid and there was just something about a blue-collar guy that did it for Harper.

'This is Harper,' Brock introduced. 'She's here for Yarran.'

Six sets of eyes cut to her. The laughter and camaraderie falling silent. An older guy with a solid gut and bushy beard streaked with silver regarded her speculatively. 'Really?' It wasn't hostile but she was left in no doubt they were forming ranks around their captain.

She supposed, as Yarran's colleagues, they knew his history. And a woman turning up out of the blue *would* make them wary. 'Oh, no.' She shook her head. 'We're just friends.'

Trying to be anyway.

And maybe she should practise saying it out loud because it didn't sound very convincing even to her own ears.

'Well,' silver beard said, nodding slightly, 'any woman who brings chicken is welcome here.'

'Amen,' a redhead guy said as he snatched the bag out of Brock's hands and headed for the table and everyone seemed to relax. 'Grub's up,' he announced as he pulled the food out of the bag and plonked it in the middle of the table.

'You want to join us?' the redhead asked, glancing at her.

She was saved from answering by a door opening behind her. 'Oh, hey,' Yarran said as she turned. 'Sorry, I was on the phone.'

Harper was hyper aware they had an audience who were watching the interplay between her and Yarran but she was *more* aware of Yarran and the way her body lurched. Seeing him in uniform had always turned her on and apparently nothing had changed.

It seemed the universe just wasn't going to cut her a break.

'It's fine,' she dismissed.

'I see you met the guys,' he murmured, tipping his chin in their direction.

'She came bearing chicken,' Brock said, brandishing a leg.

Yarran looked at her then, cocking an eyebrow. 'You are such a suck-up, Jones.'

It surprised a laugh out of her. She'd forgotten he used to call her that, back in the day. She turned back to the table where the food was currently being devoured. 'Gotta support my fellow shift workers, right, guys?'

'Solidarity, sister,' agreed a guy with a beanie on his head.

'Hey, Harper,' Brock said, licking his fingers. 'You any good at trivia?'

She shoved her hands on her hips. 'Played on the winning hospital trivia team five years in a row.'

'Hospital?' Bearded guy looked at her scrubs. 'Nurse?'

She shook her head. 'Doctor.'

Everyone appeared suitably impressed and the bearded guy said, 'You're in, then. Sunday arvo.'

'I am?'

'We're one short for trivia at the Slippery Eel.'

'Ignore Riggs,' Yarran said, with a glare at the

other man. 'He doesn't know how to ask because he sucks at talking to women.'

'I heard he was still a virgin,' Brock quipped.

There were hoots of laughter as Riggs, who sported a gold wedding band, said, 'Bite me,' and bit into some chicken.

'It's fine.' Harper shook her head. 'It'll be fun. I'd love to.'

Why not? Before leaving London, she'd played regularly at the pub over the road from the hospital. Plus, that was what friends did— accepted invitations. They'd be in company and it could be a good way to establish their friendship—for them *and* for others.

So everybody could see they'd moved on and were perfectly fine spending time together and absolutely did not want to jump each other any more.

Riggs and Brock high-fived. 'We're going to kick *ass*.'

Yarran sighed and shook his head as he looked at her. 'You don't have to.'

'All good. I love trivia.'

'Okay, great…thanks.'

His smile seemed a little fixed though and Harper wasn't sure *he* wanted her there. 'So…' she prompted. 'My wrap?'

'It's in the car, out the back. C'mon—' He gestured to the stairs. 'I'll show you.'

Harper nodded. 'Thanks.'

'Leave me some chicken, you douche bags,' he threw over his shoulder.

'We're making no promises,' Brock said.

Harper waved at the guys. 'Bye. Nice meeting you all.'

'See you Sunday,' Riggs said.

CHAPTER FIVE

THEY HEADED DOWN the stairs as the ruckus of smack talk resumed. When she got to the bottom he directed her around behind the stairs to where the door to the engine bay was located, opening it for her.

It was a voluminous space, dominated by three bright red engines gleaming under the downlights as if they'd just rolled off the factory lot. The chrome dazzled and the deep red of the body looked lush and glossy as cherries. It had been a long time since she'd been in a fire house, but the strong stench of petrol, grease, smoke and *nostalgia* was almost overwhelming.

Yarran pointed left. 'Back door down there.'

Harper spotted it but she didn't move. 'Which is your engine?' she asked. She knew firefighters rode on all vehicles but they were usually assigned to one engine.

He tipped his chin at the nearest. 'Number 352.'

Nodding slowly, Harper wandered over, conscious he was watching her intently. Absently, she stroked the duco of the front driver door. It looked as if it had been spit-polished, it gleamed so damn hard, and her hand glided with ease across the surface.

Yarran had explained to her once a shiny engine was a source of pride for a firefighter. Just like the shiny buttons and polished shoes of the formal uniform worn on ceremonial occasions. Firefighters needed to be in tip-top shape and so did their equipment—truck included. A dirty engine didn't inspire public confidence.

'Shiny as ever,' she said, more to herself than Yarran.

'Yes, ma'am.'

She turned to face him, her shoulder blades sliding against the duco. He was standing against the wall, his arms folded, one knee bent, the foot placed flat against the wall behind. It was a thoroughly casual yet utterly masculine pose. Emphasising the breadth of his chest, the meatiness of his quad.

He looked every inch the fireman.

'You still love it?'

He smiled and dimples softened the angles. 'What's not to love about spending your work hours with that bunch of clowns?' He tipped his head to indicate the guys upstairs. 'What about you? You still love being a doctor?'

'I do.'

'You're good. That day with Emma…it was your first day and it looked like you'd been in charge there for years.'

'Thank you.'

She took his compliment and yet, standing here in front of him, Harper couldn't deny the hollow kind of feeling that had taken up residence in her chest seeing him with his team. She felt…envious, she realised. Envious of the easy relationship Yarran had with his colleagues. Sure, she was well respected at the Central and people deferred to her, but it wasn't the kind of camaraderie that developed when you spent every shift at the coal face with your colleagues.

People didn't divulge anything to the boss.

Which was why she really wanted to make it work with her old friends. And maybe saying yes to trivia was part of that?

'About trivia…' Maybe she'd been wrong about that hesitancy she'd seen but she'd rather talk about it now than let it go—they'd done too much of that in the past. 'I don't have to come if you don't want me to. I just thought it might feel less…weird between us if we started seeing each other socially, you know, in a group sort of setting. Maybe the quickest way for us to become friends is to start acting like it?'

'It's fine.' He shook his head. 'It's a good idea.'

'You seemed hesitant…'

'No, I just… You were put on the spot. I wasn't sure if you were being polite.'

'I wasn't,' she assured him.

He didn't say anything for a beat. 'I do want you to come.'

There was an intensity in his voice and his gaze that caused a tiny little skip in Harper's pulse and emphasised the brooding masculinity of his foot-against-the-wall stance.

'Okay, good, well…that's settled.' She pushed away from the truck. 'I better let you get back to the guys.'

Dropping his foot to the ground, Yarran headed for the back door. Ever the gentleman, he opened it for her, pushing down on the bar, the loud clunk echoing around the engine bay. Harper was careful not to brush against him as she exited the building, which was no easy feat when the aroma of Acqua di Gio stirred heady memories.

Spying his car, Harper crossed the parking space. They didn't say anything, their footfalls on the gravel the only sound in the whole car park although the more distant sound of traffic could also be heard.

Removing his keys from his pocket, Yarran activated the door unlock and they thunked open as the parking lights flashed twice. Harper reached the car, leaning her butt against the back door as he opened the front passenger door. Leaning inside, he opened and shut the glove box before straightening and turning to face her.

'I don't think it got too crumpled,' he said as he passed it over.

Harper took it, one end of the narrow silky sheath escaping to trail on the ground. 'It's fine,' she dismissed as she hauled in the errant tail, winding the fabric around her hand. 'Thank you for finding it. I don't really wear that dress often so it probably would have been ages before I realised it was missing.'

'You should wear it more often. You looked amazing.'

She glanced up to find his gaze fixed on her and she was glad for the solid weight of the car behind her. They were close, she realised. A bolt of heat struck her deep and low as another waft of his cologne made her a little dizzy and just like that, she was back in his car Saturday night, the air in her lungs hot and heavy.

'A well-designed dress can make anyone look amazing,' she dismissed.

He chuckled and it was all low and warm. 'You never could take a compliment.'

Harper opened her mouth to object but shut it again. It was true, there was no point in denying it. Praise had been in short supply where she'd grown up and she'd learned to regard it with mistrust. It had taken some time getting used to Yarran's easy compliments.

His eyes roved over her hair and she wished she could look away but their dark interest was as compelling now as always and she wished it were falling around her shoulders, soft and shiny like his fire engine, instead of hanging limply in some end-of-shift bedraggled ponytail nightmare.

'Green always suited you.' Yarran's gaze returned to hers.

Yarran had said that many a time. And standing here in this car park it was as if all the years between them evaporated and they were the way they'd always been after a night out together, revelling in the low buzz between them, the tug in her belly as strong as ever.

'God, Harper...'

He shook his head slowly and she was too afraid to press him for more or ask what he meant because she knew.

'One of these days I'm going to see you and not want to kiss you,' he muttered, his gaze dropping to her mouth. 'But this is not one of those days.'

He took a step in and Harper's breath hitched, her pulse a living, breathing thud inside her head. Wanting it. Not wanting it. Knowing they *couldn't* keep doing this. Knowing they had to ignore this insane chemistry if they were ever going to be friends.

She shut her eyes as his hands slid either side of her face, trying to block out the temptation of his face, of his mouth.

'You looked so damn good against my truck,' he muttered, the warmth of his breath caressing her face. But he didn't kiss her, he just pressed his forehead to hers, their noses brushing, their lips close. Oh, so close.

The raggedness of his breath mixed with the raggedness of hers.

'Yarran,' she whispered, her hand sliding over top of his, sensing he was hanging on by the same thread she was. 'We can't.'

It took a beat but he heaved in a deep, shuddery sigh. 'Yeah,' he said, his voice like gravel as his hands slid away and he took two steps back. 'C'mon.' He shoved his hands in his pockets. 'I'll walk you out.'

Harper followed him on very wobbly legs, wondering how many near misses would it take before the dam broke and the *can'ts* became *why-nots?*

* * *

Harper hurried into the busy beer garden of the Slippery Eel on Sunday afternoon. She hated running late but traffic had been a nightmare with everyone, it seemed, heading for the popular beachside suburb of Manly to enjoy the last of the warm weather before winter really made itself known.

Of course, she'd also changed three times…

Scanning the bench tables, at the end of one she spotted Riggs, who waved her over. Because half of the table was hidden behind a central bar area, she couldn't see the other end, but as she made her way through and around the crowded area more of the table came into view and she recognised quite a few of the guys from the station on Wednesday night.

It wasn't until she was almost at Riggs's side she could see all ten occupants, including Yarran, who was sitting at the opposite end.

With Jarrah on his lap.

She'd seen the pictures of him, of course, and even if Harper hadn't known either of them from a bar of soap, she'd still know they were father and son. Jarrah was a mini-me version of his father. Gorgeous brown skin, dark curls, dark eyes and, as he smiled at something his father said, two wicked dimples.

A rush of something she couldn't identify flooded her chest as Yarran looked up and their gazes locked. Knowing, logically, Yarran was a father was one thing—seeing it in action was entirely another. It looked *good* on him.

'Glad you're here,' Riggs said. 'It's starting in fifteen.'

Harper turned her attention to Riggs but was excruciatingly conscious of Yarran's gaze on her profile. 'There's table service and a menu down there.' Riggs tipped his chin towards the other end of the table. 'We saved you a seat.'

'Down here, Harper.' Brock gestured, sliding down the bench seat a little to make room for her at the end. Which put her immediately to Yarran's right.

Yarran smiled at her tentatively as she made her way down. It seemed half welcoming, half apologetic and maybe because she was already feeling a little blindsided at the unexpected tumble of her emotions, it made her kind of angry.

He didn't have to apologise for bringing his kid to a social outing, for crying out loud.

Plastering on a smile, she said, 'Hey,' to Brock then turned to Yarran. 'Hey.'

'Hi,' he said, causing Jarrah to look up from his colouring to regard her with those eerily familiar brown eyes. So like his father's. So like his aunty! He smiled then and, *holy crap*, those dimples.

'And you must be Jarrah,' she said.

He looked puzzled in that comically inquisitive way only small children could pull off. 'How you know my name?'

'Because I'm a friend of your daddy's.'

It felt awkward saying it. *It felt like a lie.* But right there in front of her was the reason why they had to stay friends. Yarran had a son. He'd moved on, and he had other responsibilities. A child to think about. To put first. 'That's right,' Yarran agreed. 'This is my…friend. Harper. She's Aunty Li-Li's friend as well.'

His eyes went large, as if knowing Ali were magic. 'You know Aunty Li-Li?'

'Yes, I've known her for a long time. We're old friends.' She crossed her fingers under the table.

'Did you know my mummy?'

Yarran's swiftly indrawn breath covered for Harper's surprise. But she recovered quicker as Yarran gaped at his son. 'No, I didn't. But Aunty Li-Li tells me she was *great.* And I know she loved you and your daddy very much.'

In truth, Harper didn't know any of those things. But she knew *Yarran*. And, on another level, she knew how it felt to be motherless. She knew the ache of that absence and how she'd held onto her mother's whispered *I love yous* through all the back and forth of her childhood because they'd trumped *everything*.

Her terrible choices. Her poor coping. Her inability to manage at life.

As a child, knowing she was loved by her mother had been more important than the actual mothering. Every kid should *know* that.

Harper met Yarran's gaze and for a moment they just stared at each other. 'Thank you,' he mouthed over Jarrah's head.

She gave a small shrug. She might not be the most maternal woman on the planet but she wasn't a complete novice with kids either. The gaze held for a beat too long before she broke it to return her attention to Jarrah.

'Now, let me guess,' she said. 'You're...nine years old, right?'

He laughed. 'I not nine. I three.' He held up two fingers. 'Almost four.' He put up another finger.

'And do you want to be a fireman when you grow up, like your dad?'

'No.' He shook his head. 'I want to be a policewoman like my mummy.'

Harper nodded, ignoring Yarran's flinch. 'Fantastic. I bet she'd be super proud of you.' A quick glance at Yarran told Harper he wasn't quite ready to enter the conversation. 'Whatcha colouring in, there?'

'It's all the things I gonna has at my party,' Jarrah continued, switching out a yellow pencil for a blue pencil, not noticing his father's stillness.

'You're going to have a pony?'

His eyes widened again as he looked at Harper. In a *very loud* whisper, he said, 'We gonna have an entire *zoo.*'

'Wow.' Harper glanced at Yarran with a raised eyebrow.

'A petting zoo,' he confirmed, his voice thick.

'But you can't tell no one,' he said, his eyebrows beetling as he stared at Harper with seriousness. ''Cos it's a surprise.'

'Okay,' Harper agreed solemnly and mimed zipping her lips.

Jarrah giggled, his dimples flashing. 'And there's gonna be lots and lotsa nanas.'

'You like bananas?'

'Nanas are my favourite.'

'The lolly ones?' Yarran clarified and their gazes held for a beat at the significance.

'Really?' Harper dragged her eyes off Yarran. 'They're my favourite, too,' she said, trying to keep her voice even. Yarran had always kept her in a steady supply. She held her hand up for a high-five, which Jarrah dutifully offered. 'And are all your friends coming?'

'Uh-huh.' He nodded as he concentrated on colouring between the lines.

'I'm coming, aren't I, bud?' Brock said.

Harper had been so busy conversing with Jarrah and worrying about Yarran's discomfort, she'd forgotten Brock was even there. 'Unca Brock gonna dress as a fireman for the mummies.'

Yarran, who had been taking a sip of his drink, almost spat it out as Harper turned her head and raised an eyebrow at Brock. 'Oh, really?'

Completely unabashed, he shrugged. 'Why should the kids have all the fun?'

'Daddy?' Jarrah turned a little to look at his father. 'Can Harper come to the party?'

Yarran did his best not to look alarmed, but Harper knew him well enough to see the signs. Frankly, she was feeling a little alarmed herself.

'Yeah, Daddy,' Brock added. 'Can Harper come?'

Harper vaguely noticed the narrowing of Yarran's eyes in Brock's direction but she was too busy scrambling for a way out of the invitation to kick Brock under the table.

'Oh, I don't think—'

Yarran started at the same time Harper said, 'I'm not sure…'

'Oh, *please*, Daddy, please!' Jarrah's gaze turned impassioned and his expression endearingly earnest as he gazed at Yarran. 'I gots friends and you gots friends so Aunty Li-Li should have a friend too.'

Harper would have laughed at the irony had she not been in the middle of a near panic attack. She was possibly the last person *Aunty Li-Li* would want to see at Yarran's house. And, on that, they agreed. It was one thing to be friends but another entirely to get involved in Yarran's family life again. To see his parents. His brother and sisters. People who had once upon a time been a big part of her life.

She was hoping that would come with time, not be thrust on her all at once.

'Aunty Li-Li will know everyone at the party.'

'But she wants to come, don't you, Harper?' Jarrah switched his attention to her.

Harper blinked. How did she say no to such sweet earnestness? It was as if the happiness of his entire life hinged on what Harper said next. 'Umm—'

'Please?' Harper swore the kid actually batted his eyelashes at her. Long, sooty eyelashes women the world over would kill for. 'I'll even share my nanas with you.'

'Jarrah,' Yarran said, warning in his voice, an apologetic expression on his face.

It would have been easy, she knew, to just say, *I'm working* and be done with it. But…she *couldn't*. She didn't want to see him crestfallen. As a kid who had been disappointed a lot in her life, she didn't want to dish that out to this kid.

To Yarran's kid.

She smiled at Jarrah. 'I would love to come to your party.'

'Yes!' Jarrah threw his hands up in the air triumphantly.

And then he did something completely unexpected. He threw himself at Harper. Given they were sitting at right angles and the corner of the table was in the way, it was mostly unsuccessful, but he did latch onto her arm and hug it tight, pressing his little cheek against her biceps.

She vaguely noticed that his hair smelled like apples and his skin like cookies and cream and there was something sticky on his hand before everything around Harper faded to black. The chatter from all around, the clink of glassware, their table companions—everything disappeared. It was just her and this little boy, hugging her arm as if she'd given him a year's supply of nanas.

And his father, looking on with an anguish that tore at her very soul.

Yarran's phone ringing thankfully dragged her back to the moment as he answered it with a gruff, 'Hi.' He nodded a couple of times. 'Yep…great…thanks…be right out.' Hanging up, he said, 'C'mon, mate, Granny's here to pick you up.'

Jarrah gave her one last squeeze before letting Harper go, his attention already shifted as he scooped up his paper and slid off his father's lap. 'Say goodbye,' Yarran said, collecting the pencils and shoving them in a small backpack.

'Byee-bye,' he sing-songed.

Everyone waved and Brock high-fived him then Yarran ushered him out. Harper watched them go, wondering what the hell had just happened.

'Cute kid, huh?'

Harper blinked as she glanced at Brock. 'Very.'

Too. Damn. Cute.

Yarran took a minute to gather himself as he waved Jarrah and his mother off. What the hell had just happened? He'd figured Harper and Jarrah meeting today had been inevitable when his mum had messaged to say she was running late and, in truth, he had been nervous about it.

But he hadn't expected the wild churn in his gut seeing Harper with Jarrah. Joking and laughing and chatting with him as if she was an old hand with kids. Not talking at him as if he were a baby as so many people did, just treating him as if he had something interesting to offer.

For a woman who proclaimed she didn't want kids, she'd built a quick rapport.

Still, Jarrah had thrown her—and him—some curve balls which was…not cool. Mentioning Marnie a couple of times when he didn't really speak much about her at all. And then inviting Harper to his birthday party. What on earth had possessed him to invite someone he'd known for five minutes?

Clearly, almost-four-year-olds weren't known for their executive thinking, but Yarran had not been expecting *that*. Not least because he wasn't entirely sure how he felt about having Harper at the party.

But the most shocking thing today had been that hug. Just out of the blue. Jarrah was usually more guarded around people he didn't know well so it had been a surprise to say the least—for them both, if the look on her face was anything to go by.

More than that though, it had hit Yarran in a deeply personal place. Seeing Jarrah hugging Harper had made him acutely aware of the gaping hole in his life, in his *son's* life, and, probably most shocking of all, for the first time since Marnie's death, Yarran's mind hadn't automatically gone to the woman who'd left that hole.

It didn't go to Marnie. Because it had been full of Harper, of how good she looked holding his son, of how he could get used to it, of how she'd make a great mother.

And, *Christ*, he didn't even know what to do with that…

Striding inside five minutes later, he resumed his seat near Harper. She was wearing a strappy sundress in a swirly pattern of green and blue, her auburn hair all loose and he had to fight the urge to brush it aside and drop a kiss on her bare shoulder. As he once would have done without thinking twice.

Trivia had started but his gut was still all churned up and the need to apologise for what had transpired rode him hard. She'd barely acknowledged him arriving back at the table but she hadn't looked comfortable being put on the spot by a kid—*his* kid—so it was the right thing to do. She was participating in a whispered discussion over whatever question had been asked just prior to him entering the garden but it wouldn't take long.

'I'm sorry,' he murmured as he leaned towards her. 'About Jarrah putting you on the—'

Turning to face him abruptly, she scrunched her brow. 'What's a funambulist do?' she asked, cutting him off. 'I think it's a tightrope walker, but Riggs thinks it's someone who collects matchbooks.'

Her gaze locked with his and he got the message loud and clear. She did *not* want to talk about this now. Or maybe ever, given Harper's tendency towards avoidance.

'I'm not sure,' he said, trying to clear his head of the jumble of thoughts and emotions. 'But I don't think it's matchbooks.'

'It's gotta be the tightrope thing,' Brock whispered. 'Fun and ambulist—right?'

Riggs's eyebrows beetled together. 'It's too obvious.'

Harper, who had turned her attention back to the table, shook her head a little. 'I can't be certain, but my gut tells me I'm right.'

'Hmph.' Riggs regarded her with his unflinching stare. 'How often is it right?'

She stared right back, also unflinching. 'Almost always.'

He pursed his lips for a second. 'Okay, then.' He wrote the answer down. 'Just so you know, you get this one wrong, you won't be asked back.'

Yarran could tell Riggs was just yanking her chain but only because he'd known the man for over a decade. 'Ignore him,' he said, addressing Harper as he bugged his eyes at the guy down the other end of the table. 'Riggs takes this a little too seriously.'

'Like I said,' Brock said, whispering conspiratorially, 'Riggs is a virgin.'

Which cracked everybody up, but Harper just shook her head. 'No, no. I like it. I get it.' She nodded at Riggs. 'I *respect* it.'

'Oh, God,' Brock said, looking from Harper to Riggs then back to Harper again, feigning horror. 'There are two of them.'

More laughter ensued but the next question was asked and the team dug in for the remainder and it was *so* nice watching Harper laughing and smack-talking with his friends. It was nice seeing her unguarded and then miffed when the team—the Fireman Sams—was just pipped at the post.

'Jesus, you two.' Brock shook his head at Riggs and Harper, who were triple-checking their score against the other teams on the score board. 'We're not playing for sheep stations.'

'We were robbed,' Harper muttered.

'Yep.' Riggs nodded. 'We'll get them next time.'

She cocked an eyebrow and Yarran watched

the small smile tugging at her mouth wishing he were on the receiving end. 'So I passed muster, huh?'

He pointed the pencil at her. 'You're one of us, now.'

'That's right,' Brock agreed. 'You can check out but you can never leave.'

She laughed and Yarran's heart went *thunk*. Harper was really something when she let down her defences. Something she hadn't done often, except with him. And he knew that had scared her the most about them.

A large box of fun-sized chocolates was delivered to the table as their second prize and they all feasted on their reward. Harper grabbed a purple-wrapped chocolate and stood. 'My round, who's up for another drink?'

Several light beers were ordered. 'Not me,' Riggs said, also standing. 'Gotta get back. See you next week?'

Harper nodded. 'I'll be here.'

Brock offered to help her carry the drinks and they both departed. Riggs made his way down to Yarran and sat in the seats Harper and Brock had just vacated. The muscles in Yarran's neck shortened as the other man regarded him for long silent moments.

'That one,' he said finally, pointing to Harper, who was standing at the bar, laughing at Brock.

Yarran's jaw tightened. 'It's not like that.'

'Uh-huh.' It dripped with disbelief.

'We're just friends. We go a long way back.'

Riggs grunted. 'Has she got a partner?'

'No.'

'So?'

'It's too soon.'

'It's been three years, man.'

Yarran shook his head. 'I've got Jarrah. He keeps me busy enough.'

Riggs snorted. 'Yeah... I don't think you're going to have a problem with the little fella. He seemed quite taken.'

Yarran wished he could deny it, but Riggs was right—his son had taken to Harper. And she, it seemed, had taken to him. But... 'She never wanted a kid.'

'Yeah, but having your own is different from mothering one already in existence.'

Yarran didn't know. He was forty years old and she'd been back in his life for two weeks and everything was upside down. 'She's a *friend*, Andy.'

'Hmm.' Riggs obviously knew from the use of his Christian name that he'd pushed enough for one day. 'Okay.' He rose again, placing his hand on Yarran's shoulder as he passed by. 'Just so you know, you lose me this trivia partner and I'm going to leave your sorry butt stuck halfway up a ladder one day and you won't know where or when it's going to happen.'

Yarran laughed at the comically empty threat. 'Noted.'

CHAPTER SIX

HALF AN HOUR LATER, Harper had finished her lime and soda. Apart from some awkwardness there at the beginning with Jarrah, it had been a thoroughly enjoyable afternoon and it was still only just after three. The sun was shining and she had the urge to go to the beach. She hadn't been since her return and she knew within a matter of weeks it'd be too cold and she'd be completely disinclined to go.

And Manly Beach was only a five-minute walk from here. 'I'm going to go and dip my toes in the ocean,' she announced. 'Who's in?'

'Yeah, I'll go,' Yarran said.

She nodded at him, unperturbed by his eagerness. They were supposed to be old friends, after all, and there were eight others at the table. Except no one else, it appeared, wanted to go, declining one after the other. And it would be hard to backtrack in front of everybody because why wouldn't she want to go to the beach with her *old friend*?

So, as everybody departed for their vehicles, she and Yarran walked out of the back gate of the beer garden. She could have changed her mind after everyone had left, begged off with some forgotten chore, but she supposed they should talk about the whole party invite thing.

Plus, now the urge had struck, she really *did* want to wriggle her toes in the sand.

They didn't talk much as they made their way to the esplanade navigating around family groups and other clumps of people on the main street. In his white T-shirt, floral boardies and flip-flops, Yarran looked casually sexy and way more appropriately dressed for the beach than she was, but Harper was liking the sun on her shoulders.

An ice-cream truck was parked on the grassy foreshore in the shade of a towering Norfolk pine, just one of the many dotting the sea frontage. Yarran brought two chocolate-dipped soft serves.

'Thanks,' Harper said as he passed hers over. She bit into it and sighed as the chocolate made a cracking noise and sweetness burst like rainbows across her taste buds.

They headed for the esplanade where one railing and a drop of several feet were the only things separating them from the sand. The beach wasn't as crowded as it would have been earlier and most people were concentrated in the area around the yellow and red flags.

The turquoise ocean was relatively calm, waves breaking close to the shore giving swimmers something to play in, while a line of surfers rode the swell out further. Two jet skis traversed the bay further out again, their jets of water spraying in an arc out the back. Laughter floated on the light breeze along with the cry of seagulls squabbling over old chips.

'Looks cold,' she mused as she pulled up at the railing and leaned on it.

'Nah.' He shook his head. 'This is perfect swimming weather.'

Harper glanced at him sideways just in time to see him take a swipe of his ice cream—a long slow lick with the flat of his tongue, which brought back a hell of a lot of very *non-friendly* images. She glanced quickly away. 'You always did have the pelt of a seal.'

'You're just a cold frog, Jones.'

She opened her mouth to object to the name but licked her ice cream instead. Yes, it was a nickname, but it was a friendly one. It wasn't an endearment. Not something lovers called each other.

'If by that you mean I prefer not to turn blue

when I get in the water, then guilty as charged.' She smiled at him sweetly. 'C'mon, I want to get some sand between my toes.'

Kicking her flats off, she carried them in one hand and the ice cream in the other. Yarran followed suit and they took the nearby concrete stairs down to the beach, heading in the opposite direction to the clump of beach-goers. The sand still held some of the warmth of the day beneath her feet as Harper licked at her ice cream.

'So…what does one get a four-year-old for a birthday present? I'm guessing a teddy bear is too young and a scientific calculator is a little too old?'

'I really am sorry about him springing it on you like that.'

'It seems like he sprung it on you as well.'

'Yeah.' He chuckled. 'He did.'

'I don't have to go if you really don't want me to. I just…didn't have it in me, to say no, not when he was pleading with those big brown eyes of his that look…'

She didn't finish the sentence but Harper felt his long, assessing glance almost as a physical caress and had no doubt he knew exactly what she'd been going to say. 'Yeah,' he said eventually, 'he uses them to good effect.' And then after a beat, 'I don't mind you coming to his party. The more the merrier.'

Harper was down to the cone now and she bit into it and crunched while she gathered the courage to voice the next question. 'And your folks,' she asked. 'Will they mind?'

'Of course not.' He shook his head. 'They'd love to see you again.'

'So, they're not angry with me?' Strands of hair blew across her face and she shook her head to remove them. 'Like Ali?' Harper had adored Lyn and Coen, which had only made her decision to leave harder.

'My parents were disappointed. *For me*. No parent wants their child hurting.'

Harper tried not to flinch. Yarran was talking generally, she knew, but it spoke volumes about their vastly different childhood experiences. Her mother's actions had caused a lot of hurt in Harper's life—intentional or not. Harper truly believed if it had been within her mother's powers to stop her self-destructive behaviour then she would have.

But some people, as her great-aunt had said, weren't equipped to deal with life.

'They were just old enough and wise enough,' he continued, 'to know that sometimes in love you win and sometimes you lose and that's life. Ali is just…' His eyes strayed ahead as he bit into his cone. 'She feels what I feel, you know?'

'Yeah…' Harper pulled herself away from old,

old memories. 'I know.' In truth, it had always freaked Harper out a little. Never having had a sibling, she found the synergy Yarran and his sister shared wholly unrelatable.

'They know you're back and Mum asked if it was okay by me if they invited you over in the next couple of months, so I'm pretty sure seeing you at the party will be a treat.'

'Oh.' A little flutter of relief flared to life in Harper's chest as she nibbled around the edges of her cone. She knew she'd burned bridges when she'd left—some almost irreparably—but maybe some had only been a little singed. 'And is it okay by you?'

'Of course.' He smiled. 'We're friends, right?'

She nodded and smiled back, a little flutter of hope in her chest. 'Right.' If anyone had cause to despise her it was him. And yet, he didn't.

He finished the rest of his cone in two bites while Harper continued to savour hers in small nibbles as they walked with nothing but the sound of the waves between them.

'Thanks again for what you said to Jarrah. When he asked if you knew Marnie.'

Harper shrugged. 'Of course.'

'He doesn't mention her much any more so it kind of surprised me.'

'Is it hard?' she asked, feeding the last bit of

the cone into her mouth before continuing. 'To hear him talking about her?'

'Not at all.' He shook his head. 'We all try and talk about her as much as possible. He has a photo of her by his bed and we have a couple more scattered throughout the house. I know he doesn't remember her so I want to be able to keep her alive any way I can. I just—' he sighed '—want him to know how much Marnie loved him.'

Harper slowed and turned to face him. His voice was clouded with doubt, as if he wasn't sure what the hell he was doing. But, from where she stood, he was putting his kid first and prioritising love and that was all Jarrah needed. 'You're a good father, Yarran.'

He stopped too, shoving a hand through hair made even more unruly by the wind, the fabric of his shorts blowing against the muscular definition of his quads. He gave a half-laugh. 'It doesn't feel like it a lot of days.'

'Oh, yeah?' She smiled to lighten the moment as she also brushed hair back from her face. 'What *does* it feel like?'

'Like I'm one of those rats running on a wheel while simultaneously trying to juggle a dozen pieces of cheese and having them constantly fall on my head.'

Harper laughed. 'You never were much of a multitasker.'

He laughed too. 'I can face a fiery inferno without thinking twice and then I walk through my door and Jarrah smiles at me like I'm his whole world and he depends on me for *everything* and—' He blew out a breath. 'I wasn't supposed to do this alone.'

'He just needs you to love him, Yarran. To put him first. Take it from someone who knows.'

Their gazes locked. He regarded her for a beat then gave a slow nod. 'Yeah.'

Harper broke eye contact at the sudden rash of goose bumps prickling at her arms. Absently, she rubbed her hand up and down her forearm to quell their march. 'Ugh.' She glanced at her hands. 'Sticky.'

Tossing her shoes on the sand, she headed for the ocean, aware Yarran was following her at a slower pace. She stopped as the water lapped at her feet and almost yelped at how cold it was. The weather might be going through an unseasonably warm patch but, as she had predicted, the ocean hadn't got the memo.

Gathering up the skirt of her cotton dress as she crouched, Harper dipped her hand in the incoming wash, shocked anew by the frigid sea water.

Yarran crouched beside her. 'See, I told you,' he said. 'Positively balmy.'

Harper had no idea what devil made her do what she did next. Maybe it had been the heaviness of their conversation. Maybe it had been the remnant of that earlier lightness she desperately wanted back. 'Oh, really?' she said sweetly, then scooped up a handful of positively balmy ocean and splashed his face.

He shut his eyes on impact, his face frozen for a second before they blinked open, staring at her. *Yeah, not so balmy now, buddy.* But then his expression changed and a frisson of something that was both primal and sexual flared at the base of Harper's spine.

His dark eyes widened. 'I'm going to get you for that, Jones,' he growled.

Harper didn't know whether she should be amused or turned on, but she knew she should *run*. But not before she splashed him again. 'You gotta catch me first.'

He roared as he lurched after her and Harper squealed as she sprinted up the beach, away from the water, her hair and her skirt flying behind her.

'I'm going to dump you in the ocean when I catch you.'

'Oh, yeah?' she threw over her shoulder. 'Talk's cheap.' Harper knew she had no chance of outrunning him, particularly in the softer sand, but, *God*, it was fun trying.

It was…exhilarating and she felt *giddy*.

He was soon on her, as she knew he would be, and she dodged and weaved, laughing so hard she almost fell over, but within the next few seconds he'd snagged a handful of her hem to slow her, then reel her in.

'Gotcha,' he crowed.

She laughed and panted and twisted to try and get away—she wasn't going to make it easy for him—but eventually he had her, their bodies colliding. Their feet got tangled as she squirmed though and she started to topple, grabbing for him as she went. But all she succeeded in doing was bringing him down with her and they both landed in the sand in a tangle of limbs, laughing and out of breath.

It took probably longer than it should have for it to sink in that Yarran was half on top of her, although her body was intimately aware. One thick thigh was thrust between her legs, high and hard. His chest was half across hers, his forehead pressed to her cheekbone, his silky hair caressing her temple, his nose brushing the angle of her jaw, his lips dangerously close to that sensitive point just behind her ear.

Hot puffs of his breath fanned goose bumps down her neck as a low buzz in her pelvis made itself known and Harper's senses filled with the essence of Yarran and the freshness of Acqua Di Gio. It was heady and dizzying and Harper felt like her most primal self as she turned her head slightly to inhale.

'You still wear the same cologne,' she said, her pants more ragged than when she'd been running full tilt.

What she should have said was, *Get off me, you great big lump.* That would have been wise. It would have been sensible. But everything pulsed and hummed and buzzed and he felt so good like this, chest to chest, and she was almost out of her skin with wanting him.

She was far, *far* beyond wise and sensible.

He lifted his head, his eyes roving over her face as if he was cataloguing all the changes twelve years had wrought and liked what he saw. He was also distractingly out of breath.

'Why ruin a good thing?' he murmured huskily as he fingered a strand of her hair, lifting it to his face, rubbing it against his cheek before letting it fall.

His gaze drifted to her mouth then and Harper's belly squeezed and her lips parted involuntarily, and she was pretty sure she made some kind of noise at the back of her throat because his eyes widened and he muttered, 'God help me,' under his breath then lowered his head and kissed her.

And it felt like coming home.

His lips glided over hers, slowly at first, thoroughly, as if he was relearning the contours, then became more demanding as desire sparked like an inferno between them, raging under her skin, scorching her from the inside out. That resolve she'd had at the fire station the other night to resist this *burn* between them also going up in flames.

He groaned and it reverberated straight into her bones as his hand swept down her body, landing on her hip, pulling her closer, their bodies perfectly in line now. Their ragged breathing in sync. The pound of his heart pounding in time with hers. And it didn't matter that they were *very publicly* making out because all that mattered was this man, big and hard and so much a part of the fabric of her life, kissing her as if they'd never been apart.

The facts there was going to be sand in places that shouldn't have sand or anyone on the beach could walk by and see them weren't a concern either. Hell, they could have an entire audience *grading* their performance and Harper couldn't have cared less.

She just needed to be closer.

Draping her leg over his hip, she moaned as

the hot, slick centre of her came into intimate contact with the hot, hard thrust of him.

Closer. She needed to get closer.

Sensing her need or perhaps just responding to his own, Yarran slid his hand to her ass, holding her tight, his erection pressing at just the right angle over sensitive flesh. Even with several layers of fabric between them it felt so damn good she moaned again, her fingers fisting in his shirt.

'Yarran,' she muttered against his mouth, her voice not much more than a rasp. 'I need...' She rocked against him, desperate to be *closer.* 'I need...'

'I know,' he panted, 'I know.'

He rocked then, too, and Harper realised he *did* know. He knew exactly what she needed because he needed it too.

Closer.

And God alone knew how much *closer* they might have got but for the sudden urgent wail of a siren slicing through their cocoon of intimacy.

They startled apart, Harper's ragged pants and the loud wash of her pulse through her ears almost obliterating the god-awful noise. 'What the hell is that?' she asked, looking around, confused as to why an old-fashioned air-raid siren was echoing around the beach.

Yarran fell back against the sand, a hand on

his abdomen, his breathing as ragged as hers. 'Shark sighting.'

Even though her body was still in an absolute uproar, Harper somehow managed to glance over at the flagged area. Lifesavers in their iconic yellow and red ran into the shallows urging people in with loud speakers. Not that anyone needed it as everyone hurried for the safety of the beach.

'There's a shark?' she asked absently, a strange kind of disconnectedness descending.

One second, she was dry-humping Yarran in full public view and the next there was a... shark? Could there be *anything* more Australian?

'Maybe,' he muttered, his eyes firmly fixed on the sky overhead.

Harper also fell back against the sand, still too discombobulated by how they'd ended up making out *again* to be able to compute that there might be some large predator stalking swimmers. Had she been that way inclined, she might be tempted to believe there was some kind of divine intervention going on to keep them apart.

She wasn't but perhaps she'd do well to heed it, anyway. It seemed stupid to look a gift shark in the mouth.

'Saved by the shark,' Yarran muttered, still staring at the sky.

The urge to laugh hysterically pressed against her vocal cords but she quelled it. 'I think it's a sign.' One that reinforced what they'd already agreed on—staying *friends*.

He sighed. 'Yep.'

'I should go.' It was a statement that didn't come out with a whole lot of conviction because there was a stubborn part of Harper that didn't want to move a single inch.

'Think I'm just going to...lie here for a bit.'

'Okay.' Rousing herself, she sat, putting her skirt to rights and dusting the sand off the backs of her arms and out of her hair. Then she pushed to her feet, walking to where they'd discarded their shoes and scooping them all up.

He hadn't moved when she returned to his position and tossed his shoes down. Given the vastness of the beach surrounding them, she'd have expected Yarran to look dwarfed but his presence was as virile as ever, lying there, his eyes hot on hers. How was it even possible for him to look just as potent horizontal looking *up* at her as he had looming *over* her?

Maybe it was the way his gaze ate her up or the very definite bulge in the front of his shorts. Either way, if she didn't leave now she might be tempted to do something about that bulge that could well get them arrested for indecent exposure.

Harper swallowed. 'See you later.' And she departed without waiting for a reply.

The sound of children's laughter greeted Harper the following Saturday afternoon at four-thirty as she followed the instructions on the hand-painted sign festooned with balloons and made her way around the side path of Yarran's house. It had been almost a week since she'd seen him and her pulse kicked up in anticipation.

She'd made up her mind on Wednesday morning to ring him that night and make an excuse for not being able to go to Jarrah's party, but then Ali had attended the department for an emergency placental abruption on Wednesday afternoon and commented on how Jarrah hadn't been able to stop talking about Harper attending.

And she hadn't been able to do it.

She did, however, decide to set some mental boundaries, going forward. *After the party.* Like restricting their time together to Sunday trivia, only. This way they got to progress their *friendship* but in a very controlled environment. A public place. Plenty of people around. And also, no more sexy dalliances on Manly Beach!

No more sexy dalliances, full stop.

The party was in full swing when Harper stepped into the backyard. She was late because she hadn't known what one wore to a four-year-old's birthday party. Even settling on the casual midi-dress with a square neckline and a tight shirred bodice, she still wasn't sure she'd got it right.

Streamers hung from every branch of every tree occupying the neat garden beds and fairy lights criss-crossed the yard from the balcony railings to the railings of the pool fence. They were on but the full effect wouldn't be able to be appreciated for a couple of hours yet.

Individual helium balloons on plastic sticks had been poked into the top of the hedge at the back fence to spell happy birthday and, just in front of the hedge, a table groaning with food had been set up. In the far left back corner was the petting zoo and several children wearing party hats were sitting on hay bales tending to an assortment of animals. One held a rabbit, another a fluffy yellow chicken, the other was patting a tiny goat. Several more were stroking a Shetland pony as a handler hovered nearby.

Other children chased each other around the yard, flitting between groups of chatting adults, while others bounced merrily on a large round trampoline, fully enclosed in a mesh safety net. Wally watched the proceedings from the deck, his ears pricked.

Harper spotted several of the guys from trivia as well as Ali and Phoebe chatting near the table of food. Ivy had been called in to the Central and hadn't been able to attend. Yarran, looking far sexier than a man wearing a pointy party hat should, was talking to his parents.

Harper's stomach flopped over. It had been twelve years since she'd seen Lyn and Coen, but they hadn't changed a bit. Yarran's father was still tall and broad, with a calmness honed from decades as a paramedic. And Lyn, ex-Olympic sprinting champion, still boasted a mix of grace and athleticism from years of physical training and her indigenous heritage.

Coen said something and Yarran and Lyn laughed, her hand sliding around her husband's waist in obvious affection. Harper had always laughed at the combined groans of the family over their parents' public displays of affection, but she had personally *adored* Lyn and Coen's closeness and a familiar rush of envy lanced her right through the middle.

There was so much *love* in this backyard. Yarran and Ali had been lucky to grow up in such a loving family. So was Jarrah.

Harper glanced away, spying Brock in the middle of a group of women. One was laughing as she placed her hand on a bulging biceps, testing out its firmness. Brock's youthful charm clearly didn't have an off button.

'Harper!'

She started at the sudden excited exclamation as Jarrah burst forth from a clutch of kids and barrelled towards her. She was conscious of curious looks as he threw his arms around her legs. 'Oh.' Harper froze for a second, momentarily at a loss as to how she should act, especially with what felt like the entire party population waiting for her next move.

'Hey…bud.' She patted him awkwardly on his back as the hug continued. Did he greet everyone with such enthusiasm? Or was he just tripping on a nana high?

He pulled away and looked up at her, his hat sitting atop his wild mop of curls. 'You gotsa come and see my pony.'

'Ahh…' She looked around, unsure as to the right protocol for a children's party. Should she give him his present first? 'Okay.'

'Jarrah, let poor Harper get in the door first.'

Lyn. Harper looked up as she approached, smiling that genuine smile of hers, and the tension that had worked its way into every muscle in her neck eased. Lyn Edwards didn't look as though she was holding any grudges.

'Hey, you.' She grinned and it was big and clearly sincere. 'It's *so* lovely to see you again.' And then she pulled Harper into a big hug.

Harper shut her eyes on a wave of emotion. Lyn had always been free in her affection with

Harper and tears pricked the backs of her eyelids as she relaxed into the familiar hold. It had taken her a long time to get used to such open fondness but she'd sure as hell missed it.

When her eyes blinked opened again, she could see Coen approaching with a similar look of welcome. But it was Yarran bringing up the rear she was most aware of. He wasn't frowning like Ali, but he wasn't smiling either, and she wished she could read his mind.

Was he also feeling a weird sense of déjà vu?

'Long time no see,' Coen said as he joined them, also reaching for a hug.

'It's been a while,' Harper admitted, her voice muffled in his shoulder.

He patted her on the back a couple of times. 'It feels like yesterday.'

'Ha!' Lyn snorted as Harper eased out of Coen's embrace. 'Apart from these ruts in my forehead and the grey hair.' She poked at the fine lines, clearly annoyed at their presence.

'I adore your ruts,' Coen said with a smile, earning him an affectionate eye squint from his wife before turning his attention back to Harper. 'How are you settling in? I bet it's like you never left.'

Harper couldn't look at Yarran lest everyone see that, where he was concerned, it definitely felt as if she'd never left. 'Settling in well,' she confirmed. 'My apartment will be ready next week so that will help.'

'Is that my present?'

Harper glanced at Jarrah, who was shifting from foot to foot. He'd been very patient letting the adults get reacquainted. 'Yes.' She handed it over and hoped like hell he liked it.

Unprompted, Jarrah said, 'Thank you,' and ripped off the paper in three seconds flat.

It was a small terrarium with an African violet sporting one lone purple flower. He looked at it quizzically and Harper chewed nervously at her bottom lip. It wasn't exactly a toy—you couldn't *play* with it.

'Wow!' Coen said to his grandson. 'A terrarium. That's awesome.'

Jarrah studied the glass bowl as if he wasn't entirely sure. 'Daddy…' She stumbled over the word. It was still strange thinking of Yarran as *daddy*. 'He said you liked to help him in the garden so I thought it might be nice to have an inside plant?'

'That's a great idea,' Yarran concurred.

Jarrah, however, didn't look convinced. *Good one, Harper. Buy the kid a dud present, why don't you?* She suddenly wished she were anywhere but here under the scrutiny of a bunch of people who probably *didn't* suck at kids' birthday presents while being judged by a newly minted four-year-old.

Yarran's newly minted four-year-old.

A sudden desperate urge to be liked by him spurred her on. 'And…see those pebbles? They glow in the dark.' She'd remembered Yarran saying he was afraid of the dark and thought it would be a super-cool alternative to a night light.

Or maybe some horrible triffid nightmare… *Crap.*

But suddenly, Jarrah's eyes lit up as he gazed at her. *'Really?'*

God…those eyes. 'Cross my heart.'

'Daddy!' He turned those excited eyes on his father, his expression bordering on wonder. 'Glow-in-the-dark rocks!'

Yarran laughed. 'That is *super* cool.'

'Thank you, Harper,' he said, his voice hushed with awe. 'I gots to show Sammy.'

He took off then as if he were holding the Holy Grail and everyone laughed, but Harper felt utterly unsure of herself. Which was ridiculous. She was the head of ER. She could crack open a chest and perform open heart massage if needed but a four-year-old's birthday present had her totally bamboozled.

She shot an apologetic smile at Yarran. 'I'm sorry, I didn't know what to get him.'

Yarran frowned but it was his mother who

spoke first. 'What? No.' She shook her head. 'It's a *great* gift. Really thoughtful. It'll last longer than half of the plastic crap he'll be getting today.'

'It's perfect,' Yarran assured her, his eyes warm. 'Really.'

She met the sincerity of his gaze with appreciation and opened her mouth to thank him but before she got anything out, a *'Daddy!'* rang out from the opposite side of the yard and Yarran gave a low chuckle.

'Sorry, Daddy duties. Gotta go.'

Daddy duties. He hadn't rolled his eyes or grimaced—he'd just laughed indulgently and gone eagerly to his son. It did funny things to her equilibrium to see Yarran *the father.* Also stirred the murky pit of guilt she carried where he was concerned. She'd have denied him this—fatherhood—had she stayed.

And *that* would have been a tragedy.

'Come on,' Lyn said, squeezing her arm gently, and Harper dragged her attention back to the other woman, whose gaze was kind, as if she knew Harper's thoughts weighed heavily. 'Let's introduce you to some people.'

CHAPTER SEVEN

HALF AN HOUR LATER, Harper had met every single person at the party and been reacquainted with Yarran's other sisters—Kirra and Marli—and she was now chatting with Ali and Phoebe, who hadn't moved from near the snacks table. Wally occasionally barked up on the balcony as kids dashed hither and thither, some even splashing around in the nearby pool under close adult supervision. Jarrah had brought her a hat and insisted she wear it, with which Harper had dutifully complied, and maybe it was the hat, or maybe it was that most people didn't know her here, but she started to relax and enjoy the atmosphere.

Even more so when conversation turned to work and, inevitably, Emma Wilson. Given the complexity of the case and the public interest due to her husband's celebrity, there was quite a buzz around her and the babies at the Central.

'She's what?' Harper asked as she bit into a lolly banana. 'Twenty-seven weeks now?'

'Twenty-six plus six days,' Ali confirmed.

'Tough enough for a single pregnancy to survive, let alone a twin birth,' Phoebe added.

'Yep.' Harper nodded.

'The babies appear to be doing well though, despite the continuing fluid and ventilation challenges for Emma.' Ali also grabbed a few bananas from the bowl and chomped one in half.

'I saw yesterday's ultrasound report,' Phoebe agreed. 'Twin two is slightly smaller than expected but still just within parameters and neither are showing signs of distress.'

'I would think with all that sedation it'd be pretty chill in there,' Harper said.

Phoebe laughed. 'True.'

'Seriously though.' Harper's gaze was absently following Yarran as they talked. Between attending to Jarrah and the other kids and mingling with their parents, he was working the party like a pro. 'Are either of you worried about the long-term effects on the twins of any of the drugs being given in ICU?'

'Not really.' Ali shook her head. 'Emma was well into her second trimester when the thermal injury occurred so the babies were essentially fully developed. And they're avoiding benzos and opiates for sedation. But who knows? It's not like we see these cases every day. Not a lot of precedent to study in literature.'

'I guess not.' Harper nodded as a woman and her partner approached Yarran. She smiled and rubbed his arm briefly before her face scrunched in something akin to concern.

'Doesn't he get sick of that?'

Harper glanced sharply at a plainly irritated Phoebe, who was also watching Yarran, her eyebrows beetled. 'Sick of what?'

'Having all those bloody sympathy arm rubs. He's not a…pet.'

Ali shrugged. 'People feel extra bad for him today. But they don't want to mention the elephant in the room.'

Harper blinked. The elephant in the room?

'Right,' Phoebe muttered with a shake of her head. 'Like this is the first time he's woken up and *not* thought, great, another day I have to be teeth-achingly happy for my son on his birthday while being excruciatingly aware the woman who gave birth to him on this day will never be around to celebrate it.'

It dawned on Harper then. The *elephant in the room* was Marnie.

And she felt terrible. She'd been concerned about herself and how she was going to face him after their beach make-out and worried about seeing his family again and fretting over the birthday present without any thought to how difficult this day must be for Yarran.

How bittersweet.

Celebrating the joy and miracle of Jarrah's birth while knowing the person who'd grown, nurtured, birthed and loved their son *first* was gone for ever. It must take an enormous amount of fortitude to *bear* a day like this, let alone throw a party and *entertain*.

Harper watched as the woman chatted away but Yarran's gaze drifted, landing on Jarrah, who was laughing as a mother belonging to the little boy standing next to him, guided his arm back and forth to show him how to make a bubble come out of an enormous wand.

A wonky bubble finally squeezed out and Jarrah grinned in excitement, looking at the other woman as if she were some kind of bubble whisperer, and the flash of raw anguish Harper saw in Yarran's gaze in that unguarded moment whammed her in the chest. It only lasted a nanosecond before he covered it up with a broad grin, but she felt its impact all the way across the yard. The expression—*his pain*—squeezed at her windpipe.

Was he thinking that the random mother should have been Marnie? That Jarrah had been ripped off? Short-changed? That'd *he'd* been short-changed? Had he just been faking his smile today to cover the great yawning hole in his life?

Harper wished she had a magic wand she could wave and bring Marnie back. For Jarrah so he could *know* the love of his mother. And for Yarran. Even though her own feelings for him were complicated, Harper had only ever wanted him to be happy.

And that, she realised now, had played a huge role in her leaving twelve years ago. Because he'd deserved someone who loved him unreservedly. He'd deserved Marnie. And if she could have filled that hole for him—and for Jarrah— right now, she would have.

'They mean well,' Ali said, her quiet musing breaking into Harper's thoughts.

Phoebe sighed. 'I guess. But I bet he's going to shut the door on them tonight, turn some music up real loud and scream at the top of his lungs.'

Ali laughed. 'Probably.'

Harper laughed too because the images of the friendly polite host working the party just now and a grown man screaming into a void of loud music were so at odds, and yet Yarran had always sworn by the virtues of loud music.

'He always said metal was good for railing against the fates,' she agreed.

Ali frowned a little and Harper got the distinct impression she wasn't ready for any affectionate forays into the past. She might have been able to get past the hurt Harper had inflicted, but she hadn't forgotten.

Thankfully, the mood was interrupted by the ball of energy that was Jarrah. 'Aunty Li-Li.' He grabbed his aunt's hand. 'Come and watch me ride the pony.' He reached for Harper's hand. 'You, too.' His little hand slid into hers and he tugged.

A tug Harper felt on the inside as well. Hell, she felt it all the way down to her toes.

'Yeah, yeah.' Ali rolled her eyes adoringly at her nephew but held her ground. 'Where's my kiss from the birthday boy first?'

Jarrah mimicked his aunt's eye roll. 'I kisst'ed you already.'

'You're four now, you gotta kiss me four times. It's the rules.'

The boy regarded her through suspicious eyes. He clearly smelled a rat. 'I heard it was the birthday boy who was supposed to get four kisses?' Harper said, her heart full at the obvious love between Ali and her nephew.

Jarrah's eyes widened. 'Yeah!'

'Hey.' Ali frowned playfully at Harper, which made her feel even lighter. 'Whose side are you on?'

'The birthday boy's, of course,' she said with a grin.

'Oh, well, then…' Another exaggerated eye roll from Ali. 'If you insist.' She hauled him in, wrapping her arms around him. 'Better pucker up, birthday boy,' she said with a faux growl. 'I'ma coming in.'

Jarrah squealed and squirmed as Ali planted tiny kisses all over his face. 'Stop, stop,' he protested as he laughed and wiggled and giggled.

Ali relented only when she'd considered him thoroughly kissed and Jarrah tugged on both their hands again. 'C'mon,' he urged, 'it's my turn on the pony.'

And, conscious of Yarran's gaze on her from across the yard, Harper could no more have resisted that tug on her hand than she could the tug around her heart.

The fairy lights in the yard started to glow around six as the party broke up. Hyperactive children with party bags in hand were protesting as they were led away by their parents, while the petting zoo people packed up. Harper had tried to leave half an hour prior when Ali and Phoebe had departed to go on to other engagements, but Jarrah had pleaded with her to stay and watch him do tricks on the trampoline, so she'd stayed.

And then, as she'd supervised several of the

kids all bouncing around, Lyn had approached and asked a favour.

'Can you stay for a while after the party tonight?' she'd asked. 'It's a bit of a birthday tradition that Jarrah has a sleepover at our place and he gets to stay up and watch his favourite movie with us on his pa's big-screen TV, then we do morning-after birthday pancakes the next day. But… I worry about Yarran being alone.'

Harper's gut clenched. *Oh, no. Please, Lyn, no.* Why her? He had plenty of friends who could keep him company, surely?

As if the other woman had read her mind, she said, 'He refuses all company no matter who I try to set up, but when we bring Jarrah back the next morning, he always looks…*dreadful*. Very hungover. And I can't help but think if he had something other than a bottle of whatever around, it might give him something else to think about.'

'Lyn…' Harper understood what she was saying but she didn't think her hanging around would have the desired effect. 'I'm not sure my company helps.'

'I disagree. Having someone who *wasn't* around when it all happened might just be the ticket. Besides—' she gave a wry smile '—he's much too polite to kick *you* out.'

Lyn might be right on both accounts, but she

didn't know what had been going down between the two of them these past few weeks. So Harper had opened her mouth to politely decline. But then Lyn had touched her arm and said, 'Please, Harper. Just for a bit?'

And she was sunk. Harper always had found it hard saying no to Lyn and tonight had been no exception. It seemed as though the whole darn Edwards family had her wrapped around their little fingers!

So here she was out under the fairy lights picking up the toys scattered around the pool deck and placing them back in the basket. Lyn and Coen and a few others had stayed behind to help clean up the yard and kitchen but they'd left with Jarrah—clutching his terrarium—twenty minutes ago and everyone else had departed soon after. Yarran was outside somewhere seeing off the petting zoo people so Harper had the backyard to herself.

With the party all cleared away, it was still and quiet now, just the trill of evening insects. She leaned on the top rail of the pool fence, draining her beer as she watched the lights winking on in the houses beyond the back fence. She'd never pictured Yarran in suburbia, and yet he was clearly thriving. The house was welcoming, the yard was immaculate and, given how many neighbours had been at the party, he was clearly well liked.

If she'd stuck around, would this have been their life? Harper couldn't imagine it, but strangely, it wasn't a panic-inducing thought.

A car door shutting out on the street roused her from her reverie and her gaze fell on the trampoline. Some kind of toy was lying discarded on the mat and she wondered if it belonged to Jarrah or one of the other kids.

Letting herself out of the pool gate, she placed the beer bottle on the nearby garden edge before making her way to the trampoline. The teddy bear looked old and well loved, which meant there'd no doubt be a parent looking for it soon enough. Unzipping the safety netting, Harper tried to bounce the toy closer but only succeeded in bouncing it further away.

Resigned to fetching it out, she climbed the ladder, pulling her dress out from under her knees so she could crawl to the middle, the trampoline giving easily under her weight. Harper couldn't remember the last time she'd been on a trampoline so instead of backing out once she'd scooped it up, she flipped over and took a moment to breathe in the evening air.

It was surprisingly nice just lying here in the lazy hush of a suburban Saturday evening, purples fading to black. Stars winked to life although the fairy lights and the glow from the house prevented her from getting the full celestial display. As if the universe had heard her thoughts the house and fairy lights went out one after the other.

'Hey up there,' she said as her eyes adjusted, hundreds of stars popping overhead.

'Harper? Where are you?' The house lights flicked back on.

She could hear the frown in Yarran's voice as she rolled her head to look up at him. Wally was by his side, lapping up an ear scratch. 'On the trampoline.'

There was a pause for a beat or two. 'Did my mother harangue you to stay?'

Harper laughed. 'Yes.'

She could hear his sigh drift all the way down from the balcony. 'Sorry 'bout that.'

'It's fine,' she assured him. Even though it wasn't. But she'd agreed so there was no point complaining. 'Turn the lights out again, will you? I can see the stars so much better.'

The lights flicked out and Harper's eyes adjusted again, finding even more stars as he clomped down the stairs then padded towards her across the grass.

'Mind if I join you?' he asked as he reached the ladder.

She knew she should say yes. Should get off the trampoline and go inside where she would be in his house, surrounded by a life she hadn't been a part of and where she wouldn't be so damn *horizontal*. She could make coffee and they could eat left-over birthday cake and talk about the weather and then she could get the hell out of Dodge.

But his mother's concerns, her *'Please, Harper'* ricocheted around her brain, so she simply said, 'Sure.'

Harper rocked a little as Yarran climbed onto the mat and made his way to the centre. She shifted to give them each some space but with their combined weight forming a dip in the middle of the trampoline the sides of their bodies touched whether she liked it or not.

Unfortunately, Harper's body liked it—a lot.

She didn't know if he was as acutely aware of it as she, but he at least seemed inclined to ignore it as he pointed. 'Southern cross.'

Harper nodded. 'Uh-huh.' And then neither of them said anything for a while, they just lay there, staring up as the sky went from indigo to black and more stars appeared.

She wondered what he was thinking. Was it about Marnie and Jarrah and the emotional gut-wrench of this day? Or was he thinking about the many birthdays to come and the other milestones to come in Jarrah's life where his loss would be constantly compounded?

'Don't be mad at your mum.'

'I'm not.'

'She means well.'

'I know. I just…it's nice to be alone after having to be so *on*. It's exhausting having to assure everyone I'm fine.'

'And are you?' she asked, her voice quiet and tentative in the night.

He paused. 'Mostly.'

Harper fell silent. She supposed, given it had only been three years, *mostly* was pretty damn good. 'It must be hard for you,' she said eventually, probing some more. 'This day.'

She wasn't sure this was a Lyn-approved topic of conversation. Yarran's mother had hoped she'd be a distraction from his past—not hold a mirror up to it—but Harper knew enough psychology to know sometimes people wanted to talk, they just needed an opening.

He shrugged. 'It is what it is.'

Harper felt that shrug down the whole side of her body making her excruciatingly aware of his heat and hardness. Forcing herself to concentrate on their conversation, she conceded Yarran wasn't really giving her any openings so she decided not to push.

'How did you find seeing my mum and dad again?'

'Oh, it was…lovely.' Harper happily picked up what he'd put down as she rolled her head to look at his profile.

He chuckled but didn't look at her. 'I told you it would be okay.'

'Yeah, yeah.' Harper returned her attention to the sky. 'They haven't changed a bit.'

'Apart from the ruts in the forehead.'

Harper laughed. 'I should be so lucky at your mum's age to look that young.'

Shaking his head, he said, 'She hates them.'

'I can't believe Kirra has *four* kids.'

'Neither can I. But I love that Jarrah has so many little cousins all living nearby.'

He didn't say *in lieu of siblings*, but Harper knew intuitively it was what he meant. 'Yeah, he's lucky.'

As soon as the words were out, she could have bitten off her tongue. She shut her eyes briefly, mentally castigating herself. On today of all days, she had to go and say something so asinine. 'I mean—' Her eyes flashed to his profile again. 'I meant—'

'It's okay…' He rolled his head to the side, too, his gaze meetings hers. 'I know what you meant. He *is* lucky in lots of ways. His mother died…' Yarran's voice turned husky '…but he has so much family and love around him in this little village of ours. Sure, they're big and loud and over-compensating…' He gave a rueful smile. 'But that's not nothing.'

This little village of ours.

She'd been part of that village once upon time. And now here she was again, on the outside looking in—her nose pressed to the windowpane. The next words slipped out of her mouth without much thought. 'I wish I'd had a family as loving as yours.'

'Yeah.' He nodded slowly. 'I wish you had too.'

A slight smile touched his mouth before he turned back to the stars and they returned to contemplative silence as the heavens winked above them. Harper wasn't sure how long they lay like that, but it didn't feel stretched or awkward. And maybe that was the lasting legacy of their long-term relationship—they didn't need to fill the silences.

'Can I ask you something?' Yarran said eventually.

'Sure.'

'You don't…' He hesitated. 'Don't have to answer if you don't want to.'

A prickle shot down Harper's spine. 'Okay.'

'How did it feel…to grow up without a mother?'

Okay, well…she hadn't expected him to go there. It said a lot about them that they were together for eight years and he didn't know the answer to that question nor feel okay even broaching the topic over a decade later. He *had* tried to get her to talk about it in the beginning, but she'd been close-lipped and he'd eventually stopped asking.

'I know you grew up in the foster system so it's not the same thing. But loss is loss and… the *mother* is such a profound figure in a child's life. And I look at you and you're this amazing, articulate, intelligent go-getter and yet I know there's a little girl in there somewhere that suffered.' He rolled his head to the side, his gaze meshing with hers. 'That still suffers, I think. And I can't…bear the thought of it.'

Harper knew he wasn't probing for himself. He was asking *for Jarrah*. He couldn't bear the thought of his son suffering. And it clawed at her gut to know he was willing to push against a wall he knew only too well was gnarly with vines and practically immovable, to get answers. To be best prepared for his kid.

Like a true parent.

So perhaps it was time to be moved. Maybe that was something she *could* do for Yarran after all these years. Give him answers. For Jarrah's sake. And hadn't she been thinking that sometimes people just needed an opening?

Yarran waited, unsure if Harper would answer. Would finally go there. The fact she hadn't got up and left was encouraging, but that didn't mean she wouldn't, which was cranking up his anxiety.

She was right, today *was* a hard day—how could it not be?

But Harper's presence had, for the first time since Marnie's death, managed to take his mind off the fact she was no longer here to celebrate the special day. Being excruciatingly aware of Harper's every move from the moment she'd stepped into the backyard instead of the weariness of grief and the hovering scrutiny of the people who loved him had made the day so much more bearable.

Even more so, watching her go from clearly anxious standing there in that knockout dress, clutching that present looking as if she wanted to flee, to supervising kids on the trampoline— laughing and joking and rubbing banged heads and soothing bruised egos—had been marvellous.

And the way she'd been with Jarrah? Wearing the party hat he'd bequeathed her as if it were a tiara and letting him drag her all over. Not to mention the absolute genius of her present—one she'd obviously put a lot of thought into. She'd remembered Jarrah liked to garden and that he slept with a night light.

She'd always been thoughtful and watching her morph into the old Harper—the Harper he'd loved—had been just what he'd needed, today. And now here she was, breathing huskily into the night, seriously contemplating— he thought—talking about a subject she'd *never, ever* wanted to talk about.

'My mother…'

Her voice was halting and Yarran swore he could actually hear her swallow. Out of some instinct he couldn't put a finger on, he reached for her hand. With their arms jammed together, it wasn't hard to find. When her cool fingers curled against his, he gave a light squeeze and she continued.

'She died when I was nine.'

Yarran blinked, turning his head to look at her. 'Oh…' That he hadn't expected. 'I'd assumed she'd died when you were much younger.' He'd assumed that was the reason she'd been fostered.

'Nope.' She didn't look at him, just kept her gaze fixed overhead. 'She was an addict. Functional for a long time. Until a few years after I was born when things really started to go off the rails. That was the first time they took me away from her.'

The first time? Yarran closed his eyes.

'I bounced back and forth for the next six years. She'd get clean and… I'd go back.'

'Sounds very…disruptive.'

'It was. But I *wanted* to go back. She was my mum. I loved her. She loved me. I *know* she loved me. She might not have been very good at managing life but those times we were together, when she was first clean again, they were *happy*. We weren't rich and I didn't have a lot of stuff but she had the sweetest laugh. And she always cut my school sandwiches into different shapes. I never knew what I was going to get when I opened my lunchbox.'

She laughed and, despite how sad it sounded in the night, Yarran could feel how much Harper had loved her mother.

'I know that if it had been within her power to change, she would have. But…some people just aren't equipped to pull themselves up by their bootstraps.' She shook her head. 'God, I hate that phrase. She was a victim of gross multi-generational family dysfunction. Not many people come back from that.'

'No,' he agreed, 'they don't.'

'I was in a temporary foster home when she overdosed. The social worker came and told me and I remember just being...numb. I remember them telling me it was okay to cry but I *couldn't*. I think I always knew it was the way it was going to end and I was just...' she gave a harsh half-laugh '...pissed off to be right.'

Yarran squeezed her hand harder. He hated that Harper had been through such hardship but, more than that, he hated that she'd borne it all alone. He hated that he hadn't pushed her more about this when they were together—maybe he couldn't know her pain or take it away, but he could have listened. He could have wrapped her up and hugged her as he wanted to now.

'I'm sorry,' he said.

'Thank you.'

'And I'm sorry I didn't ask these questions all those years ago.'

She turned her head and their eyes met. 'You tried.'

Yarran nodded. He had. But... 'We were together for eight years. I should have tried harder.'

'No.' She shook her head. 'I was too used to burying it by then. Too frightened to show anyone my scars in case it was too much and they left.'

'I wouldn't have left.'

'Of course. But...everybody left so...' She looked back up at the stars. 'I know it doesn't make any sense. It doesn't make much sense to me either. It's not about logic though, it's about a very deep, very old wound and the mental lengths a child goes to for emotional protection.'

God. No wonder he hadn't been able to unpick that narrative.

She squeezed his hand. 'It's okay, I don't blame you for not pushing me. I was pretty good at shutting you down.'

Oh, yeah, she'd been an expert at that. And as much as he'd wanted to know her story, he'd known then and he knew now, he wasn't *entitled* to it so he'd always let it drop when she'd made it clear she didn't want to talk.

'I debated pushing for more all the time.' Hoping that one day he'd ask and she'd *want* to tell him. 'But I didn't want to lose you either.'

'And you would have.' She rolled her head to look at him. 'If you'd pushed too much, I would have walked away earlier. My flight instinct was always well honed.'

Yarran nodded. 'Yeah.' So he'd dropped it—every time.

As they both returned their attention to the stars, he thought about their eight years together and which moments he would have been prepared to give up to go into the fray with Harper.

None of them. Not a single one.

'Did you go to her funeral?' he asked after they'd been silent for a long time.

'Yes. Me and my case worker and some of my mother's friends from NA.'

The bleakness in Harper's voice painted a picture more vivid than any words as he examined her profile. He didn't say anything, just waited for her to continue.

'I don't know how many foster homes I went to over the next few years.'

'You weren't given a permanent foster placement?'

'Ah, no…' She shook her head. 'I was angry and…well…suffice to say, I wasn't exactly a treat of a child. But when I was in grade nine, a great-aunt of mine—Jacqueline—turned up out of the blue and I was with her for two years.'

Yarran frowned. 'She just turned up?'

'Yep. I know it sounds incredible but she was estranged from her family for many years, which is unsurprising given what I know about my mother's family. I'm pretty sure Mum never knew she existed. She lived in the UK for twenty of those years and it was only when she got back that she found out about Mum dying and me and…' Harper shook her head. 'She just kind of swooped in and it was—' she sighed '—wonderful. Like…nirvana. She had this quirky apartment and all these pictures of London on her walls and for the first time in my life I actually felt like it was all going to be okay.'

Oh, God. He didn't like the sound of that. 'What happened?'

She didn't answer for the longest time and Yarran watched Harper's profile as it ran the gamut of emotions. Her throat bobbed and he swore he heard her swallow. 'She died of a massive heart attack playing golf when I was at school one day.'

'Oh, God… *Harper.*'

Yarran's lungs felt too tight for his chest. How much was one person expected to bear? Turning on his side, he drew her hand up, kissing the knuckles absently before tucking it against his chest.

'It's fine,' she said eventually but she still didn't look at him and if she'd registered the brush of his lips, she didn't acknowledge it. 'I had two amazing years.'

Fine? It was *awful.* Even worse was Harper's low expectations, as if she'd never thought her good fortune was going to last, anyway.

'She used to say to me, "Listen, girlie, life's dealt you a crappy hand and I wish I could go back and change that but I can't. I *can* tell you the only way you don't end up like your mama and my sister and our mama before us is to get the best damn education you can. I wish I could tell you I had the money to help but I can't tell you that either. You are, however, whip smart and that's what scholarships are for."'

Harper laughed then, as if she was caught up in a memory. 'She'd shake her finger at me and say, "You got that, girlie?" and I'd nod and she'd tell me she was proud of me and even though I ended up back in the system again afterwards, I worked my arse off to get a full scholarship for her. For me, too, of course, but mainly for her.'

Yarran had known she'd gone to uni on a full scholarship, but this extra information had given him new insight into why she'd busted her ass at uni. God knew she'd cancelled numerous dates with him in deference to studying.

'So…yeah.' Harper blew out a breath, the rush ruffling some strands of flyaway hair at her temples. 'Growing up without a mother sucks. In an ideal world every child would have two loving parents, but you and I both know that's not the way it goes.'

She turned her head finally to look at him and their gazes meshed.

'Whenever I think about my mum, despite her being what was quite a disruptive influence in my life—unintended or not—it feels like a piece of me is missing. Like something vital. An organ or a limb. It's not as acute as it used to be but it's still there. And yeah, Jarrah will probably always feel like that too, even though he won't necessarily understand it because he won't have any tangible memories of her. But he has an amazing support system around him—big and loud and overcompensating as they may be.'

She smiled then and Yarran smiled back.

'And kids need that more than one parental figure that's been held up over centuries as the *ideal*. They need unconditional love and absolute protection from someone they trust and there doesn't have to be a *mum* for that.'

She looked away, her eyes turning back to the sky as she drew in a long shuddery breath. 'Sometimes,' she said, her voice husky, 'there can be a Great-Aunt Jacqueline.'

Yarran watched as a tear slid out of the corner of her eye, slowly trekking to her temple. Her voice was utterly desolate and even though they were so close they were touching, she looked so damn alone. And he couldn't *bear* it.

Levering himself up onto his elbow, Yarran stared down into her face. Her gaze shifted from the sky to his meet his, blinking up at him through twin puddles reflecting sorrow and starlight. Yarran's heart tore in his chest as another tear spilled.

'Oh, love,' he whispered, his hand slipping from hers to cradle her face, his fingertips funnelling into her hair. 'I'm sorry.' His breathing was rough, as he kissed the tear from her cheek. 'I'm so, *so* sorry.'

He kissed the other side, sipping up another, his pulse a slow, thick thud at his neck. Then he kissed all over her face—nuzzling her eyes, her nose, her forehead, her ears, the corners of her mouth, murmuring, 'I'm sorry,' each time his lips touched down.

Cool fingers slid around his wrist, encircling it. 'It's fine,' she replied, her voice rough and low. 'I'm fine.'

'I know,' he said as he pulled back slightly to stare into her eyes again. He'd never met a woman who held herself together more. Which was why her tears *eviscerated* him. 'But don't you ever want to feel more than just fine?'

Her eyes roved over his face as if she was mapping it in the dark. Or maybe re-familiaris-ing herself. Her hand slid from his wrist to his jaw, up his cheekbone, to his forehead, plough-ing into his hair and pushing it back. 'Yes.'

CHAPTER EIGHT

YARRAN KISSED HER THEN. Properly. On her mouth. Gently, not seeking or probing, just holding, his pulse a water hammer through his head. Then she moaned, her hand gliding to his shoulder as her mouth opened, allowing him in.

Past her lips. Past her walls. Past a dozen years of absence.

And he took it, tentatively though, the slow side of his mouth on hers soft and seeking rather than hard and conquering and it was familiar in all those good ways. But it was new, too. Breathy and tremulous, straining at the leash, caught somewhere between enjoying the moment and the brink of possibility.

Her moans whispered their delight through his head, they stroked against his body and fizzed like pop rocks on his tongue. She tasted like birthday cake and beer—who knew that was such an intoxicating mix? She filled up his senses until he was dizzy.

A little too dizzy for his own good.

But, even caught up in the slow turn of her mouth and the low burn of arousal heating his muscles to jelly, he knew he was far too melancholic tonight to just *make out*.

'God…' he muttered, breaking their lip lock. He pulled back slightly, his heart thumping behind his ribcage, the warm, husky rush of her breath calling to him. 'I wish—' He dropped his forehead against hers, not sure what he wished at all now, just too *overcome* with her. With *Harper*.

Harper back in the country. Harper back home. Harper back in his life.

'What?' she whispered. 'What do you wish?'

He gave a half-laugh. 'I don't know exactly.' That they'd never been apart. But then he wouldn't have had those amazing years with Marnie. He wouldn't have Jarrah.

Maybe that they'd parted differently? Without so much left unsaid.

Lifting his forehead, Yarran took her in again, his thumb stroking against her temple. 'I wish I could kiss you without wanting more. I just… don't think I can. Not tonight.'

'Maybe that's our problem,' she murmured. 'We've been trying to ignore this chemistry between us, telling ourselves *no*, hoping it'll go away.'

'Yeah.' Yarran nodded slowly. 'That hasn't really worked, has it?'

She shook her head. 'So maybe we should let it burn out in one flash of heat?'

Yarran's breath hitched at the suggestion. A very sensible suggestion. One that sank into his bones in all its profound glory. *One flash of heat.* Blood surged anew through his veins and arteries, heat suffusing every cell, his body going hard—everywhere.

'Maybe the better question to ask is, what do you *want*, Yarran?'

'I want you,' he muttered, his gaze holding hers, his voice low and rough. Three little words yet the relief at letting them out flushed hot and heady through his system.

'Because you don't want to be alone tonight?'

'No.' He shook his head vehemently. Being alone didn't bother him. 'Because I can't stand another second without being inside you.'

There it was. Right there. Plain and simple. And he *throbbed* with it.

Yarran swallowed. 'What do you want?'

The hand at his shoulder clutched now. 'I want you inside me more than I want my next breath. I want tonight.'

Heat and blood and sex and triumph roared through his veins. He could give her tonight. 'Good answer.' Then he rolled up on top of her.

* * *

Every pulse point in Harper's body leapt as the weight of him pressed her deeper into the trampoline mat. She parted her legs, the hard jut of his erection finding the screamingly sensitive place at the apex of her thighs. He was big and hot and heavy and she revelled in it. Revelled in the weight of him, in the way he looked at her. Lust and desire and something darker sparking in his gaze.

She wanted him, this man she'd never really shaken from her system. Except she wanted him more than ever. More than she'd thought it possible to want a man.

They'd tried denial. Surrender was the only thing left.

Harper didn't wait for him to kiss her, she lifted to him, their mouths meeting on a rush of air and a groan that sounded as if it had escaped from the recesses of Yarran's soul.

Yes. This.

This man. This mouth. The hot probe of his tongue and the slow grind of his erection hitting just the right spot. Her hands slid from his shoulders down his back to his ass, holding him hard against her as she wrapped her legs around his waist.

The movement adjusted the angle slightly and she gasped. *'Yarran.'*

He groaned. 'Need you *now*.'

And she knew exactly how he felt. Groping between their bodies, she found his fly, yanking down the zip as he rucked up the material of her skirt. It was a hasty choreography of grasping, grabbing, fumbling fingers, the thud of her pulse and their heavy breathing was the soundtrack.

He found her panties, his fingers slipping inside finding her wet and needy, at the same time she reached inside his underwear finding him hard and just as needy and they both gasped, their lips parting, staring into each other's eyes as they familiarised themselves with long-forgotten contours, fingering and fondling, their breathing rough in the night.

'I don't have a condom,' he muttered, his forehead once again pressed to hers.

'I have an implant and haven't had sex in over a year.'

He groaned as she slid her hand up and down his shaft. 'Three for me.'

Harper knew at some point that information would need to be parsed but, right now, all she saw was a giant green light. Dragging his head down, she kissed him, her tongue sliding against his as she guided the delicious hardness in her hand to her centre. She moaned at the thick nudge of him—*God*...had it always felt this good?

He thrust then, sliding in on a long groan until he was high and deep and she remembered—*yeah, it had*. It had *always* felt this good. He withdrew and thrust again, in case she needed another reminder.

Oh. God. Yes.

'Yes,' she whispered, her fingers ploughing into the hair at his nape, her heels pressing hard into his ass. '*Yes*. Don't stop.'

He didn't stop. He withdrew and entered again. And again. And again. A guttural kind of grunt spilled from his lips with each thrust, the give and bounce of the trampoline seating him deeper each time. Harper pressed her face into the side of his neck as the pressure and the stretch undid her, shooting darts of pleasure through her pelvis like fireworks in the night.

Placing the flats of his forearms either side of her head, Yarran surged over her again and again, seeming to know just the right pace and angle to rub just the right spot with his steely length. She was a moaning, mindless mess in his arms, trembling as much beneath him as he seemed to be trembling over the top of her.

'*God*,' she panted, a bright flare of sensation deep behind her belly button starting to ripple. 'Close, so close.' And it felt *right*. As if the old rhythm they'd had wasn't lost, merely suppressed. And was now fibrillating wildly to life.

Without missing a beat, his mouth left hers, his hand yanking at the shirring of her bodice, pulling it down, exposing a naked breast and its rapidly burgeoning nipple to the cooling night air before he took it in his hot, hot mouth and sucked.

Hard.

It was like a bolt of lightning, a flaming arrow straight to her core, the bright flare blowing out, her orgasm rushing forward, swamping her in a blink. She gasped, every part of her pulsing, from the flutter of the tiniest arterioles to the thick pound of her abdominal aorta to the rhythmic squeeze of her centre clenching around the rigid thrust of him.

Harper twisted her fingers in the hair at his nape as she came apart. *'Yarran...'*

His mouth left her nipple to claim hers, licking up her pants and her gasps and her cries, intoxicating her with his taste and weaving magic with his tongue. His pelvic thrusts slowed inexorably, teasing and prolonging, dragging in and out, stoking her to new heights.

She opened her eyes as the pleasure rained down anew, the stars overhead a blur as she shuddered and trembled in his arms. But now he was shuddering too, his biceps quaking, his breath coming in short, sharp puffs.

'Harper.' Yarran grunted, the piston of his

hips discordant now. 'I can't... I need...' He breathed hot and heavy into her neck as he hunched over her, gathering her close.

'Yes,' she murmured, her orgasm shifting in intensity as he switched up the angle and pace of his stroke once again. *'Yes.'*

He cried out then, his mouth pressed into her temple as he came, his breath hot and harsh, his thrusts turning wild, shuddering against her as he found his bliss until there was nothing left and he collapsed on top of her, the trampoline bouncing beneath them.

'I don't think this is what your mother intended when she asked me to stay,' Harper said, trying to drag in some oxygen beneath his boneless, sated weight.

'I wouldn't be so sure,' he panted then laughed into her hair.

When Yarran's eyes blinked open the next morning it took him a few seconds to get orientated. He was in his bedroom—yep, Jarrah's dyed-pasta mobile he'd made at kindergarten was hanging from the hook in his ceiling. But something felt different.

Internally.

The usual heavy feeling inside his chest, that dark cloud in his heart, wasn't there. Sure, it had lifted over the last year or so but every morning, upon waking, he still felt the weight of it. He still woke thinking about what he had lost.

But not today.

He squinted against the harsh morning light blasting in through the open curtains he usually drew before getting into bed and that was when he became aware of a warm body beside him and everything came rushing back.

Harper.

He turned his head to find her facing him, his sheet pulled up to her chin, her red hair spilling over the pillow next to his, her face relaxed in slumber. Snatches of their night together came back to him as the long sweep of her lashes cast shadows on her cheekbones. Watching the stars together on the trampoline, her finally opening up to him about her past—her frankness, her tears.

Making love to her.

Moving upstairs for a repeat performance. Rousing her in the night at some point with his lips trailing down her body, feeling her hand sink into his hair as he reached her slick, sweet core, encouraging him to stay and feast until she came so hard he was sure he'd have a bruise from her heels in the centre of his back. Then her returning the favour…

So much for one flash of heat.

He waited for the guilt to flood in. But it

didn't. And not just because he knew Marnie wouldn't have wanted him to feel any shame or remorse but because Harper was no Marnie substitute. She wasn't some woman he'd picked up to help him expunge three years of grief and pain. A hook-up to help him forget. A random warm body.

Despite what had happened between them, Harper Jones was woven into the fabric of his heart. And he wasn't going to feel guilty about reaching for a little comfort with her.

As if she knew he was watching, her eyes blinked sleepily open, the slumberous blast of green zapping all the way down to his toes. Like him, it seemed to take her a second or two to orientate herself before her body went very still and her eyes widened.

He could practically see her synapses firing behind those eyes, assessing the situation.

Would she be annoyed? Anxious? Would she regret it? Would she freak out?

She didn't do any of those things. After a beat or two she seemed to relax and she offered him a tentative smile. 'Guess we kinda screwed up, huh?'

It wasn't accusatory or panicked and Yarran gave a half-laugh. Well…they'd definitely *screwed*. 'Maybe. It doesn't really feel that way though.'

'No.' She shook her head slowly, contemplatively. 'It doesn't.'

She'd said one blast of heat, right? And that was what they'd done. But, hell, if he didn't want to reach for her again and pick up where they'd left off. Hell, if she didn't look as if she wanted it too as her gaze dropped to his mouth and lingered, fanning the coals of desire he suddenly realised hadn't been fully banked.

They were saved from the moment by a very loud rumble. Yarran blinked. 'Was that your stomach or mine?'

She laughed. 'Mine. I'm starving.'

'Well…' He grinned. 'We did burn a lot of calories last night.' Yarran glanced at his watch—quarter to eight. His parents were bringing Jarrah back at nine. Which meant they had time to eat. And talk.

With their clothes on and far away from proximity to a bed.

'There's a little suburban café about a ten-minute walk from here with great coffee and pastries. You want to stretch your legs?'

She chewed on her lip for a second or two. 'I should probably just go.'

'If you want. But…maybe we should talk about last night?'

More lip-chewing then another tummy rumble. 'Yeah.' She nodded. 'You're right.'

* * *

Ten minutes later, Yarran directed her to the walking path that cut a swathe through an area of bushland before skirting a large local park and onwards to the local shopping precinct. Birdsong accompanied them as people passed by also enjoying the sun's attempts at breaking through the cooler morning temps. A woman jogging with a pram. A young family with two little kids wobbling along on tiny bikes with training wheels.

Neither said anything as they walked for a minute or two. She was in yesterday's dress and he wondered how warped it was to get so much satisfaction seeing her in it *today*. Knowing it was because she'd spent the night with *him*.

'So…' she said eventually. 'I'm your first… since Marnie.'

He nodded. 'Yes.'

'And you feel…guilty?'

'No.' He glanced at her sharply. 'I always thought I might the first time, but I don't.'

'Oh. Well…good.'

She sounded surprised and he searched for clarification. 'I think if it had happened straight away or if it had been with anyone else…'

He let that drift off, shying away from where it might take him but that was the truth of it and she just nodded, as if she didn't want to dig too deeply into it, either.

'I guess I was just…ready. Marnie and I used to talk about what would happen if either of us died. We were both in high-risk professions and, as parents, you have to talk about the what ifs— to be prepared for all eventualities.'

'Yeah.'

'We both agreed there wasn't only one person out there for everyone and I know,' he hastened to assure her, 'last night wasn't about that. But we each wanted the other to be happy. For ourselves but also for Jarrah.'

'Neither of you were worried the other would end up with someone who wasn't keen on having a child in the picture?'

Yarran shook his head. 'No.' He supposed from what Harper had seen in her life, it was a reasonable question, but he knew in his bones that that was a no-brainer. 'She trusted I would put Jarrah's welfare before everything and I trusted she'd do the same.'

'As someone whose welfare often *wasn't* put first by my mother, I gotta say she sounds pretty great.'

'She was the best.' He gave a laugh. 'She was fun and funny. And I think it was the cop in her, but she just radiated a kind of calm that put anybody at ease in any situation.'

Yarran smiled thinking about Marnie now, marvelling at how easy it was to discuss her with Harper. He'd have thought it would be awkward but it felt as though the three of them were somehow inextricably linked. Without Harper, he would never have known Marnie.

'You would have liked her, I think,' he added. 'She would have liked *you*.'

'Did she…know about me?'

'Oh, yes.' He glanced at her and their eyes met. 'I told her everything about you.' Yarran returned his attention to the path. 'She'd been through a similar break-up with a long-term partner, and we spent a lot of time talking about you and him.' He gave a half-laugh. 'Kinda like therapy, I guess.'

'I'm pleased you found her. And *really* sorry you lost her. You deserve to be happy.'

'And what about you? Don't you deserve to be happy?'

'Hey, I had several orgasms last night.' She bugged her eyes at him. 'I'm happy.'

He laughed. Yeah, they'd made him pretty damn happy too. And gave him an opening. 'So, about that.'

Sobering, she said, 'Yeah.'

'It was…nice.' Which was about the understatement of the year.

She huffed out a breath. 'Yeah.'

'I was thinking…it could be extra nice to share some more orgasms. You appear to be in a pretty big deficit too so maybe we could do it again sometime?'

Yarran hadn't kissed her last night with this as an end goal. Nor had he woken this morning with the possibility on his mind. But, as they'd walked side by side like this, heading to breakfast as they'd done hundreds of times in the past, he'd thought—why not? They'd have to go slow because there was Jarrah to think of but maybe with time they could find their way back to each other.

The thought shimmered and twisted like a sunbeam in front of him.

'I don't know, Yarran. I'm only just back and I'm trying to make a new start—new job, new place. Find someone to talk to about all my… stuff. It's very, *very* tempting—' She grinned at him. 'But I think friends is probably the best option for us now.'

Yarran nodded, unsurprised Harper was, once again, the hesitant party. 'Of course.'

The fact she was actively talking about getting some therapy and recognising it wasn't good to muddy those waters with a new/old emotional entanglement was a good thing. A sensible thing.

'I guess we could do—' she shrugged a bare shoulder '—occasional…benefits.'

He cocked an eyebrow. 'Oh, I see. You just want to use me for sex, Jones?'

'Maybe? Occasionally.' She gave him a small smile. 'And vice versa. I just think we have a lot going on, you and I and…maybe we shouldn't make too many plans.'

Yarran wasn't sure he was comfortable with a proposal that didn't make any firm commitments, but Harper *was* right, he did have a lot going on. *And* he wasn't twenty any more. He'd learned the hard way that relationships didn't come in one-size-fits-all packages so maybe friendship with an occasional side of naked times was perfect for this stage of his life?

'Yeah.' He nodded. 'Okay. I can live with that.' He smiled then, ignoring the niggling little voice whispering *for how long* and reached for her hand. 'Come on, I can smell the croissants from here.'

She stared at his hand and, for a moment, Yarran thought she might snub it, but then she slid hers into his hold and he tugged.

Harper was feeling pretty good half an hour later as they made their way back to Yarran's house along the wide pathway. The night had been spectacular, their talk about their relationship going forward had been fruitful and the croissants were to die for—things were looking up. She had wrangled with the decision to return to Australia far more than she had with the decision to leave, but, so far, it had worked out better than she'd hoped.

The elation lasted another ten seconds, the bubble pierced by a loud, high-pitched scream followed by, '*Help!* Please somebody help me!'

Harper glanced around her in alarm, her pulse spiking at the fear and urgency in the voice. Yarran, already taking off, threw, 'It's this way,' over his shoulder.

As they rounded the bend in the pathway just ahead, Harper could see the problem. A woman was crying loudly over the inert body of a man who was lying half on the grass, half on the path. She was shaking him and yelling at him to wake up.

Yarran reached them seconds before Harper. 'It's okay, we're here now, ma'am,' he said, crouching beside her, gently trying to pry her away from the prostate form. 'What happened?'

The woman—Harper thought she was maybe in her late sixties—looked at Yarran wildly, as if she couldn't even see him. She was clearly in shock as she wailed, 'Help my husband, please just help my husband.'

Harper's attention was already on the man

on the ground as she pressed two fingers to the carotid pulse in his neck. His lips were dusky and sweat drenched his thinning hair, running down in rivulets from his forehead. Adrenaline shot into her bloodstream, spiking her pulse and honing her focus.

Her provisional diagnosis? Myocardial infarction.

But whatever it was, he didn't have a pulse and there was no evidence of chest movement, so he needed CPR—stat.

'We were just walking along,' the woman sobbed. 'He's been having terrible indigestion the last few days and thought a walk might help. And then he just clutched his chest, cried out and fell down.'

Yep—definitely an MI.

'Heart attack?' Yarran asked.

Harper nodded, tapping triple zero into her phone then jamming it between her ear and shoulder as she positioned herself and leaned in to deliver two rescue breaths. What she'd give to have an Ambu bag, a defibrillator, a cardiac monitor, an intubation kit… Hell, she'd kill for access to a cath lab right now. But all she had was herself. And Yarran.

And she was never more grateful for his presence.

'Ambulance,' she said into the phone as the

person on the other end enquired which emergency service she required.

The other woman cried harder. 'Is he going to be okay?'

Harper moved on to the chest compressions. She'd shut everything down, her adrenaline pumping as she concentrated on what she needed to do, leaving Yarran to deal with the distraught wife.

'We think your husband has had a heart attack,' Yarran explained, which caused more sobbing as the ambulance service asked Harper what had happened in her ear.

'I have a man, possibly late sixties, collapsed from suspected MI. Not breathing. No pulse.' She rattled off the details as her hands pushed down on the centre of the stranger's chest. 'I'm an emergency doctor at the Central. I've commenced CPR.'

'There's a defib at the chemist back there,' Yarran murmured, his voice low but serious, clearly aware of the gravity of the situation.

Harper allowed herself a tiny morsel of relief as the person on the other end rattled off a series of questions. 'Get it,' she said, her gaze drilling into his hoping to convey her urgency. A defib was probably this man's only chance given the terrible stats on out-of-hospital cardiac arrest. 'Run.'

Yarran didn't need to be asked twice. He sprang to his feet and ran off and Harper thanked the universe Yarran had Lyn's natural athleticism and that they weren't far from the shopping precinct.

'Ma'am. I need you to talk to the ambulance, please, they're asking about his history.' She paused temporarily to hand the phone over but the older woman just shook her head helplessly, clearly finding it hard to function. 'Ma'am…' Harper used her ER doctor voice. 'An intensive care paramedic is on the way, but they need information I can't give them. You want to help your husband? Talk to them.'

Responding to the absolute authority in Harper's voice, the older woman took the phone with shaking hands as Harper delivered a couple more breaths before starting on the compressions again. She barely heard the discussion, concentrating as she was on the actions of her hands, pushing fast and deep on the sternum, mentally counting, ignoring the ache already niggling away in her triceps.

Another elderly woman stopped to help, comforting the other woman as they both watched on. Yarran was back within five minutes and Harper could have kissed him. 'You all right to set it up?' she asked as he threw himself down beside her.

She knew that Yarran, as a fireman, was trained in first aid and that these defibs units were designed for lay people, but it was one thing in theory and something else in actuality.

'Yep,' he said briefly, his fingers moving efficiently, unzipping the case then lifting the man's shirt and affixing the sticky pads to his sweaty chest in the spots indicated on the packaging of the pads. 'ETA on the ambulance?'

'They said eight minutes so hopefully not much longer.'

He nodded as he pushed the power button and awaited instructions from the machine. Harper stopped compressions so it could get a reading. Three young guys passed by gawking and Yarran pointed back towards the chemist. 'Go wait near the road so the ambulance knows where to come.'

They took off just as the electronic voice on the machine said, 'Shock recommended. Stand clear.'

Harper and Yarran moved back, making sure no part of them was in contact with the patient. The machine delivered a shock, the man's back bowing a little, his shoulders shrugging as the charge arced from one pad to the other.

'Analysing,' the machine said. And then, 'Recommence CPR.'

Damn it—the shock hadn't been successful.

'Can you do the compressions?' Harper asked Yarran. The most experienced person always took the airway and now she had Yarran to help, she could manage it properly.

He nodded and she shuffled around to the head as Yarran took her place, planting his big hands on the centre of the man's chest and pushing, counting under his breath.

That was when they heard the first wail of the siren.

It was nine-thirty by the time they turned back into Yarran's street, as Harper and Yarran had stayed and helped the intensive care paramedic on the scene. They'd got a pulse on their third zap just as the paramedic arrived but lost it again quickly after and she'd intubated the patient—Gary—right there on the grass.

'You did good back there,' Yarran said.

Harper, feeling wrung out now from the after-effects of adrenaline, smiled absently as she came back to their surroundings. She'd been mentally walking through every step back at the scene and calculating Gary's chances. 'I couldn't have done it without you.'

Yarran had been an efficient and effective third hand, keeping up the compression as required while she and the paramedic had worked together to stabilise the critically ill patient.

A snort blew Yarran's hair off his forehead. 'Of course you could have. Hell, Gary couldn't have picked a better place or time to collapse what with the chief of the ER at a major city hospital less than twenty metres away.'

Harper flapped her hand dismissively. 'Yes, that was fortunate.'

He grabbed for her hand then and squeezed it, halting them in the process. Harper half turned to face him, his dark eyes serious as they sought hers. 'You were amazing, Harper. Really amazing.'

Ridiculously, Harper's cheeks flushed. She was good at what she did and she didn't need praise or compliments but it felt special anyway. 'Thank you,' she said, and they just stared at each other, holding hands in the street.

After what felt like an age, he grinned. 'Turned me on a little, if I'm being honest.'

Surprised, Harper blinked, but his grin was infectious and it felt just like the old days, only better because she'd finally shone a light for him to see into all her dark places and that felt so bloody…freeing. She laughed. 'Weirdo.'

'What? Competence porn, it's a thing, you know?'

He tugged on her hand and they continued along until they rounded the curve towards his house and Harper spotted his parents' car parked outside. Ali's was parked beside Harper's, which was still sitting conspicuously in his driveway, exactly where she'd parked it yesterday.

'Oh, Jesus.' Her hand loosened from his, dropping to her side, and her pace slowed. What the hell were they all going to think?

'It's okay,' he whispered. 'It's not any of their business.'

But as they neared, they could hear the stricken, wrenching cries of a child getting louder and louder. *Jarrah*. Yarran swore under his breath and, for the second time this morning, he ran.

Gripping the strap of her handbag, Harper picked up her pace too, her adrenaline blipping again, a surge of nausea roiling through her gut. She contemplated jumping in her car and careening away but she couldn't do that to Yarran. Briefly, she wondered if she could get away with a story about her joining him this morning for a platonic breakfast together but—how did she explain being in the same dress as yesterday?

By the time she opened the front door and stepped into the fray, Jarrah was wrapped up in his father's embrace but still apparently inconsolable. His skinny arms were clinging around Yarran's neck and Yarran was hugging his son tight, his eyes closed as he rocked Jarrah back and forth.

'Hey, Harper,' Lyn greeted, her face scrunched into an expression of concern as she stroked Jarrah's back.

Coen nodded and said, 'Morning, love,' shooting her a sympathetic smile as he hovered nearby.

Yarran's eyes flicked open then, meeting hers, and she saw maybe more than he'd intended. He might not have felt guilty earlier, but he definitely did now. His eyes were awash with anguish and self-recrimination.

He closed them again. Closing her out.

Harper's gaze met Ali's next. It was stony as her eyes swept up and down Harper's dress, her lips thinning as she looked away.

'I thought…you were…' Jarrah breathed jerkily, hiccoughing his anguish '…d-d-dead too, Daddy… Like Mum… Mum… Mummy.'

Harper sucked in a breath at Jarrah's heartfelt confession. He'd seemed like such a happy-go-lucky kid the two times she'd seen him. That was the thing though, with emotional trauma—conscious or not—it lay in wait and came at you at the most unexpected times.

'It's okay. I'm right here. I'm not going anywhere.' Yarran's voice was muffled in Jarrah's neck. 'I'm right here. I'll always be here for you.'

Harper blinked at the bold statement. *What?*

Nobody could make that kind of guarantee—what was Yarran thinking?

'How about we go into your bedroom?' Lyn suggested. 'Daddy can read your favourite book. Grandpa and I can come too, if you like?'

Jarrah nodded. 'Yes, p-please.'

Harper watched as the four of them headed for the hallway, leaving her alone with Ali. Her hands trembled a little as she absently noticed Wally, sitting outside the back door, whining slightly in sympathy.

'Is he…? Does that happen often?' Harper asked quietly, her gut still churning.

She had felt completely out of her depth in the face of Jarrah's anguish. She'd dealt with many a crying kid in her job, but sick kids were different. Kids in her ER she knew what to do with. She could order a test or set a broken bone or give some medication. An emotionally overwrought kid hyper-anxious about parental death?

Not so much.

'Not usually, no,' Ali replied, stiffly. 'He told Mum last night someone at kindy the other day had apparently asked about Marnie and what would happen to Jarrah if his daddy died too. So when we got home and Yarran wasn't here…'

The accusation in her voice was clear. 'We were delayed by—'

'No.' Ali cut her off with a head shake and a glare. 'I told you he was good now.'

Harper swallowed, a dark pit splitting open inside. 'Ali...no...'

'You said, okay. I thought we had an understanding. I all but *begged* you,' she said, lowering her voice, 'to leave him alone, Harper.'

'It's not like that.'

'Oh?' Ali folded her arms. 'So you didn't spend the night with my brother?'

Harper shut her eyes briefly before facing the anger in Ali's eyes head-on. She might not have to answer to Ali in any real sense but deep down, Harper knew she had to—morally. And for the sake of their friendship. 'We're not getting back together.'

'Good,' she snapped, keeping her voice low. 'Because look what happens when he's with you. You left the country and ripped his heart out and now you're back and in less than a month you've turned his life upside again. It's not just him any more, Harper. You don't just get to pick up where you left off. You don't just get to think about yourself this time.'

If Ali had slapped her, Harper couldn't have felt more rocked back on her feet. Her pulse throbbed at her temples and her jaw ached from clenching it so tight. Ali was right—what the hell was she doing? Jarrah was inconsolable,

Yarran looked as though he'd been gut-punched and her fragile truce with Ali was in tatters.

Harper swallowed. 'You're right.' God…what had she been thinking? That she and Yarran could be friends with maybe some sex on the side and everything would be fine? Nothing had ever been that simple between them.

'I'm sorry.' *Damn.* 'What can I do to make this right?'

Ali dropped her arms by her sides on a loud sigh. 'Just *go*, Harper. Leave him be.'

The message dropped like a lead sinker in her stomach, but there was a simplicity to its devastation nonetheless. She could walk away. She'd done it before. And there was a certain comfort in the familiar.

Except… *Ugh.* It *hurt.*

Wally whined then and Harper glanced in his direction. He wagged his tail a little, looking utterly forlorn. God, she'd even caused the dog distress. Clearing her throat, she dug in her handbag for her keys. 'Please apologise to your parents for me. Tell them I was called in to work, would you?' She might be walking away but she didn't want Lyn and Coen to think she'd caused this ruckus and callously fled the scene. Even if she had.

'Of course,' came the stilted reply.

She left then, not looking back at the dog or

Ali. Not looking back at the house or the street or the suburb sign as she drove away, leaving them all behind in her rear-view mirror, tears falling unchecked down her cheeks.

CHAPTER NINE

YARRAN EASED AWAY from Jarrah, who, after several reads through of his favourite book, had fallen asleep. He crossed the room to the window, placing his hands wide on the sill as he stared out over the pool, pressing his forehead to the warm glass. What the hell had just happened?

How long had Jarrah been worrying about him dying?

The sobbed confession had been like a hammer strike to his solar plexus and Yarran still felt as if he couldn't breathe properly. Guilt that his absence had triggered such tumult for his son weighed like a block of granite on his shoulders. He should have been there when Jarrah got home, not…galivanting around with Harper. Sure, the medical emergency had been an unforeseen delay in their return, but the fact was, if he hadn't been out—making eyes at

Harper—he'd have been home when Jarrah arrived.

As a good, responsible father would have been.

Harper had said it herself—*'He needs you… to put him first.'* Well…not being home when Jarrah needed him *wasn't* putting his kid first. Jarrah was the most precious thing in his world and then Harper had come back and apparently everything in his brain had fritzed.

They shouldn't have gone out this morning. Hell, who was he kidding? He should have kept it zipped last night. He clearly couldn't multitask when it came to Harper and he had a four-year-old boy who needed his absolute attention. He shut his eyes, dropping his head between his shoulders as he silently castigated himself.

What would Marnie think of this lapse in his parenting?

'I'm sorry,' his mother said quietly as she came to stand at one side. 'We rang several times.'

Yarran's phone had been on vibrate but he hadn't felt it during the resus or even thought to check it as they'd walked back to his place. He'd known they were late getting home but he'd also known Jarrah would be safe with his parents. He filled her in on the reason for their delay and she told him about what the kid at kindy had said, which made Yarran feel worse.

Why hadn't Jarrah felt he could share that with him? Had he sensed Yarran's head was elsewhere?

'It was just the perfect storm, love,' Coen said from the other side of the bed.

Yarran shook his head. 'I *should* have been here.'

'You would have been had it not been for your good Samaritan act,' Lyn soothed.

'No.' Yarran shook his head vigorously. 'I shouldn't have gone out at all. I shouldn't have…' He blew out a breath and tried not to think about how much last night had meant. 'I should have sent Harper home last night.'

'Yarran…' His mother slipped her arm around his waist. 'You deserve a life too. We've been so worried about you for so long and you've been so…different since she's been back. Like the old Yarran.'

'She's right, son,' Coen agreed.

Yeah. She was. *He'd* felt differently, too. But… 'He's too young, Mum. He needs me to be focused on him. I'll get a life later.'

'But what if you could have both?' Lyn pressed.

Coen nodded. 'It doesn't have to be either or, Yarran.'

Yarran turned to face the bed, leaning back against the sill. Jarrah's face was relaxed now but the strands of his anguish still wrapped around Yarran's heart as if it were a bug wrapped up tight in a spider's web. 'Yeah, it does,' he murmured. 'For now.'

'Sweetie…' Lyn also turned. 'You are my son and I know you like I know my own heartbeat.'

Yarran met his mother's gaze, her eyes so like his. He swore sometimes when she looked at him intently like this he could see generations of Gundungurra and Darug women staring back at him with their wisdom and compassion.

'You have a heart as big as a lion—trust me, it can love again. I know that because after Harper it made room for Marnie. And then for Jarrah. Love doesn't divide, Yarran, it multiplies.' She squeezed his arm. 'And it's okay to want to have a life partner. It's human to want to be loved. And not just by your family but by that one special person.'

Yarran knew if he had a friend in this situation he'd be saying exactly the same thing. But this was *him* and there was too much at stake. 'She doesn't want to be a mother.'

And he had Jarrah.

'Honey…that was twelve years ago. Maybe she feels differently now? Have you asked her?'

'No.'

'Maybe you should?' Coen raised an eyebrow. 'I watched Harper with him yesterday—she was great. Hell, he didn't stop yakking about her and that terrarium all night.'

Yarran glanced at his father, surprised. And… pleased. Which only ramped up his inner conflict. Was it wrong he wanted Jarrah to like her?

'Sweetie.' Lyn squeezed his arm again. 'It's been three years and you and I both know Marnie would want you to love again. And I think you *are* in love with Harper, right?'

No. Yes. He looked at his mother helplessly. Maybe…

'I don't think you ever fell *out* of love with her,' she added.

'I…don't know how I feel.' And what did it matter? He wasn't about to take some wild punt—he wasn't twenty any more.

'Fair enough.' His father nodded. 'You don't have to. You don't have to rush into anything. But, son, she looked kinda devastated out there too and you *did* spend the night with her so I'm guessing this isn't the way she pictured it was going to end. Jarrah hysterical, you walking away barely acknowledging her. Maybe she doesn't know how she feels either, but she probably needs some assurance none of this was her fault.'

Yarran blinked. *What?* 'I don't blame her for this.'

'Good.' He nodded. 'Now go and tell *her.*' He tipped his head at his grandson. 'Jarrah's out for the count. Your mother and I will sit with him, you go talk to her.'

His father was right, of course. Whatever mess was here today, he didn't blame her for it. It was nobody's fault a man collapsed, making them late. Nor was Jarrah's current emotional fragility her fault, either. His feelings might be muddied and complicated, but he couldn't abide the thought that she might blame herself.

Suitably chastised, Yarran nodded. 'Okay, thanks.'

But when he returned to the lounge area, she was nowhere to be found. There was just Ali making herself a coffee in the kitchen.

'Where's Harper?'

His sister's shoulders tensed as a visceral blast of her simmering anger hit him in that place they'd shared from as early as he could remember. She turned to face him, cradling a mug, their eyes meeting. 'She left.'

Yarran's brow furrowed. 'Why did she leave?'

Ali's gaze dropped to her coffee. 'Something about being called into work.'

Prickles spiked at Yarran's scalp. She was lying. In all their years they'd never been able to lie to each other. They were too finely attuned to get away with it. But why would she lie? Unless… 'Ali? What did you say to her?'

'Nothing.'

'Ali!'

Her eyes flicked to his and if he hadn't already sensed it, he'd have known it from the guilt stamped across her features. It was quickly replaced by a mutinous expression. 'She tore your heart out and she stomped all over it, Yarran. You were *gutted*. I know because I felt every single second of your pain like an axe blow to *my* heart.'

Yarran gaped as his sister blinked back tears. He knew she felt his pain because he felt hers too and he knew how wrenching it was to have this kind of emotional ESP. But what was happening between Harper and him was none of her business.

'It was a long time ago.'

'Except now she's back, leaving just as much turmoil in her wake and I can't bear you being hurt again. I don't think you'll survive another broken heart at her hands. And I'm damn sure I won't. So… I told her to go. To leave you alone.'

Yarran's heart thundered like a storm in his chest, a hot gush of rage rising in him, and he really hoped his sister felt all its sharp, jagged edges because he was *furious*. Ali had always taken her *older* sister duties seriously, but he was all grown up now.

'Goddamn it, Alinta,' he snapped, stalking towards her, wanting to yell it at her with the weight of all his fury but conscious that Jarrah was asleep and his parents were probably also listening. 'You had *no right*.'

'Somebody's got to save you from yourself,' she hissed back.

God…was she kidding him now? 'Stay out of it.' He spread his hands on the island counter-top and leaned over it as she glared at him from the other side. 'When I want your help, I'll ask.'

'Save your breath,' she muttered. 'I won't help you break your heart.'

A well of frustration rose in Yarran's chest as he pushed off the bench and stalked to the back door. He fumbled for his phone in his back pocket. He had to talk to Harper. To apologise. For his sister. And for the way he'd handled Jarrah being so upset.

Wally whined as he slid the door open and stepped out onto the balcony and Yarran absently petted him. 'It's okay, Wal, everything's okay.'

He stabbed at Harper's number and shoved the phone to his ear. It didn't surprise him when it rang out. It also didn't surprise him when it rang out a second time, his frustration burgeoning with each ring. It *did* surprise him when she answered on his third attempt. He'd fully expected Harper to not answer at all, which meant he'd have to leave message after message begging for her to pick up or call back.

'Hello, Yarran.'

Despite her greeting lacking any emotion, it took all of the puff out of his sails as a wave of gratitude swamped him. He really hadn't been looking forward to talking to her voicemail for the next however long. 'Harper…*thank God*… you picked up.'

'I figured you'd just keep ringing so we might as well get it over and done with.'

Yarran swallowed at the flatness to her tone. 'I'm so sorry about Ali…she had no right to tell you to go.'

'It's fine. I understand. She's your sister. She's looking out for you.'

Her voice had turned cool and Yarran could feel her slipping away, and desperation seized him, bashing away like a tiny hammer at his temple. He didn't know what he wanted where they were concerned, but now she was back he'd never *not* want her in his life.

'It's not fine, it was—'

'It was a mistake, Yarran,' she cut in, icicles hanging from her words. 'Last night.'

'Harper. No…'

'Yes. But that's okay. It was always bound to happen. We agreed it was one flash of heat so let's just leave it at that.'

Had they agreed, though? Or had there just been a tacit acknowledgment of what was happening? And their discussion on their walk had surely changed things? 'But this morning we talked about being friends, sometimes even being the kind of friends who enjoyed benefits.'

He wasn't sure why he was making such a case for what they'd said this morning given he didn't know how to feel about any of it. All he knew was this entire conversation made his skin feel too tight, as if it were about to split wide open.

Because it felt like goodbye. *Again.*

'Yeah, I think we both know now that can't happen.'

She didn't mention Jarrah's meltdown but it was obvious she was alluding to it. 'What happened with Jarrah wasn't your fault, Harper. What happened between us last night had nothing to do with this morning.'

She didn't say anything for several interminable beats of time. And then, 'I think it's best we just let it be.'

The coldness in her voice almost sucked Yarran's breath away. It was chillingly convincing and he wished he could hit rewind on the whole damn day. He sure as hell needed to speak to her face to face. Not over a damn phone line. He wanted to see her face when she told him they were one and done.

'Look… Harper. I'd like to talk to you. Not on the phone. But I can't leave Jarrah now. Can I come over sometime in the next few days?'

'No. I'm sorry, I don't want to see you again.'

And then she hung up the phone and all he was left with was the dial tone ringing in his ear.

Three days later, her words were still echoing in Harper's head. It had killed her to say it and slain her to admit it. But, even utterly miserable as she was now, she firmly believed she'd done the right thing.

Why she'd thought she could even *flirt* with the idea of having something with Yarran again was ridiculous. She'd come to start a new life, not fall back on the old, and Yarran had other responsibilities.

Thankfully it had been a busy week. Her apartment was ready on Monday and her stuff from the UK had been delivered so she'd moved out of Ivy's. That hadn't been a bad thing because Ivy knew something was up and wasn't the kind of friend who sat silently by waiting for an opening. But Harper hadn't been up to analysing it and nor had she wanted to put Ivy in the middle of something between her and Ali.

On top of that, the flu season has started with a vengeance, making the ER even busier than usual. Harper had worked late the last couple of nights and then spent several hours unpacking boxes when she got home. Which meant she was exhausted.

Yet, she couldn't sleep.

Every time she shut her eyes she saw a kaleidoscope of images from last Saturday night and Sunday morning. Yarran, his face screwed up in pleasure. Jarrah, his face crumpled in aguish. Ali, her face twisted in anger.

By five o'clock Wednesday afternoon, Harper was running on empty. Fatigue sapped every cell in her body, her eyes were bleary and she was being exceptionally irritable with her team. She was about to knock off and she was pretty sure they were all going to high-five each other as soon as she left the building.

But first—another case had just come through the ambulance bay doors. A woman who'd not long given birth to a baby girl during an assisted midwife delivery in her home, with a suspected post-partum haemorrhage. The Obs and Gynae registrar had been paged as Harper listened to the paramedic handover and the team buzzed around the cubicle getting the woman hooked up to monitors and IVs.

'Hey.'

Harper blinked, surprised to see Ali standing beside her, nodding politely and smiling at the paramedic to continue. Her registrar must be held up and they'd sent in the big guns.

The paramedics left after the handover was complete and Harper made an executive decision not to overcrowd the room. Emergency situations were fraught enough without any weird juju between the people supposed to be in charge. And they had an ace team—the head of Obs and Gynae, an ER registrar and resident as well as three nurses.

Everyone was efficient and capable. They didn't need her as well.

'I'm pretty sure you can handle this,' she murmured to Ali and turned to leave.

Ali frowned at her, flicking a quick look over Harper's appearance, her hand sliding onto Harper's forearm. 'Are you okay?'

Harper fixed a smile on her dial. 'Just peachy.'

She walked out of the cubicle and didn't stop until the greenery of the rooftop garden surrounded her. She didn't plan to leave until she knew the patient had been stabilised. Seeing Ali again had brought all the emotion of last Sunday back and she couldn't breathe.

The air was fresh and crisp up here and the garden deserted. It was a good place to clear her head. To remind herself of all the things she did have, how fortunate she was, how *lucky*. To breathe deep and give thanks for those blessings.

The rooftop garden had rapidly become her favourite place in the hospital and she'd never been more grateful for it than she was right now.

Leaning on the rail, Harper looked out over the changing mood of the city as the sun set and the lights winked on. She was truly blessed to be here, in this stage of her life—she'd outlived her mother by over a decade—and if the re-entry to Australia had been a little bumpy, then that was hardly unexpected.

And tomorrow was a new day.

Harper wasn't sure how long she stood there just breathing and letting her mind go blank but, at some point, the door behind opened. She looked over her shoulder to find Ali heading her way with an expression of grim determination.

'Everything okay with the patient?' Harper asked as Ali's elbows slid onto the railing next to hers.

'Yes. Haemorrhage has resolved and she's stable. I've arranged for her transfer to HDU overnight. They're getting a cot from maternity for the baby to room in.'

Harper nodded. 'Excellent.'

They stood for a while looking at the rapidly fading light over the city, not talking until Ali broke the silence. 'Look… I'm sorry about Sunday, I was out of line.'

Harper blinked. She hadn't expected Ali to apologise. She knew how fiercely she loved her brother. How seriously she took her role as his *older* sister. She knew they had a connection people who weren't twins could never really understand.

'It's fine.' It had been the jolt she'd needed.

'No.' Ali half turned to face Harper. 'It's not. Yarran was furious with me and hasn't returned any of my calls. It was a terrible sister thing to do. And a…terrible friend thing.'

Harper glanced at her, surprised. So, they were still going to be friends?

'Jarrah's hysterics put us all on edge and I was speaking from an emotional place. That's not an excuse, it was just where I was at. What I didn't say but *should* have was that it's been a long time since I've seen Yarran look as happy as he did on Saturday. He's been in a good place this last little while but I could still feel the *weight* in his heart. And then you rocked up to the party and he looked at you across the yard and I could feel it lift. I could feel his…*joy*. And he hasn't felt joyful in a long time.'

Ack. Joy. Why did Ali have to use that word?

She'd accepted her reunion with Yarran had been short-lived but at least their brief flirtation had left no time for *feelings*. Except, apparently, she'd given him joy. Which now she was stealing away again.

'Well…it doesn't matter anyway.' Harper returned her attention to the last golden hue gilding the building tops. 'I told him I'm not seeing him any more. It's for the best.'

Harper could *feel* the intensity of Ali's glare on her profile. 'Yeah… I can see that's working out well for you.'

Irritated, Harper turned to Ali. 'What the hell does that mean?'

'You look terrible.'

'Gee, *thanks*,' Harper muttered, wishing she could refute it.

'Are you sick?'

Harper bit back a laugh lest it come across as slightly hysterical. 'I'm just tired. Work's crazy, I've moved into the new apartment. I'm not sleeping very well.'

Ali opened her mouth to say something, but her phone rang and she dug in her pocket for it. She glanced at the screen, her brow furrowing a little. 'It's Mum.'

Harper turned back to the view as Ali took the call. 'Hey, Mum…okay… Wait… Mum… *slow down*. What happened?'

The note in Ali's voice shot an itch right up Harper's spine and she turned to hear her say, 'What do you mean, he's missing?'

Missing? A sense of dread descended. Jarrah? *Yarran.* 'What?' she demanded. 'Who?'

Ali shook her head. 'It's Harper. She's here with me now... Why was he all the way out there fighting a fire?'

Fire... Harper's breath left in a rush and she grabbed the railing for support as her legs went weak. *Yarran.* Missing. In a fire zone. The faces of every fire victim that had ever come into her ER played in full Technicolor on a loop through her head.

Harper pressed her hand to her chest, trying to try stop the pain there. Her pulse beat like a drum through her head. She couldn't breathe. Why couldn't she breathe? *God...*was she having a heart attack?

'Yes...' A nod. 'Yes...' Another nod. 'Yes. We're coming now.'

Ali glanced at Harper for confirmation and Harper nodded her head vigorously. She wasn't sure where they were going but wild horses wouldn't have stopped her going.

'What happened?' Harper asked as soon as Ali ended the call.

'He volunteered to go out to the Blue Mountains this morning to help them cover some sick leave. There was a bit of a blaze up there that took a few hours to bring under control. He's currently…unaccounted for.'

It was delivered dispassionately but Harper felt every word like a bullet and she knew Ali did too.

'Oh, God…' A sudden rush of blood to her head made her feel dizzy and *nauseous*. 'Oh, God,' she whispered, holding her side as she bent at the waist to ease the dizziness. Once it passed she levered herself upright. 'Well?' she demanded. 'Are they looking for him?'

Ali nodded, because she was blinking back tears and obviously couldn't *word* right now. Without thinking, Harper reached for her and they hugged—*hard*. 'Can you…?' Harper's voice was thick with emotion as she released Ali and looked earnestly into her face. 'Can you feel him? Is he lost or in pain or—?'

Harper cut off, covering her mouth. God… she couldn't even say the words.

'No.' Ali shook her head vehemently. 'He's not dead. He's *not*.'

A wave of relief swept through Harper—cool and full of hope. It might not be particularly scientific but she would back Ali's gut regarding her brother any day.

'You love him, don't you?'

The question was quiet but also rang with

certainty and she felt the answering ring deep inside her gut. Harper nodded. She did. 'I never stopped.'

And it felt so freaking good and awful all at once saying it out loud, finally giving voice to something she'd been suppressing for ever. She loved Yarran Edwards with her whole heart.

That was just the way it was.

'Really?' Ali's eyes probed hers. 'Cos you can't just say that and walk away if things get hard again or a little too emotionally close for you. I don't know what's happened to him but if it's something serious…' her voice wobbled a little '…he's going to need you and so is Jarrah. That's what being in love with my brother looks like twelve years down the track. He's a package deal. And even if he's perfectly fine, that equation doesn't change. So if you're in, you better be all the way in or I swear I will leave you behind on this roof.'

Harper swallowed the lump of emotion rising in her throat. Ali was absolutely right— there could be no equivocation going forward. Nor did she want there to be. She hadn't been equipped to trust what Yarran had offered her all those years ago. But there came a point in a person's life where they had to decide to be happy, to reach for that chance and trust it would be okay.

And she wanted that with Yarran. With Jarrah.

Meeting Ali's eye, she nodded and said, 'I'm all the way in.'

Half an hour later, Harper and Ali walked into Yarran's house where things had gone so wrong only a few days ago. It had been such a *low* moment but utterly insignificant now.

'Any word?' Ali asked as her parents stood and Jarrah ran to her, launching himself at her body. The television was on a news channel with the sound turned low and a radio was also on somewhere tuned to a different news station.

Lyn was clearly worried but trying to hold it together. Coen, quietly stoic, absently rubbed his wife's back. 'Nothing yet,' he said.

Smiling at Harper, Lyn wrapped her up in a huge hug. 'It's so good to see you.'

It was good to see *her*. Lyn had always given the best hugs. Coen hugged her too and tears sprang to Harper's eyes. Why had she let childhood fears deny her vital emotional support?

The next hour passed in a blur. Lyn bustled around making tea and coffee and trying to interest everyone in food. Coen flicked between news channels. Ali and Harper sat on the three-seater couch, Jarrah between them. Aunty Li-Li read to him, trying to keep him occupied. He'd been told that his father had got himself a bit lost out in the bush when he was fighting a fire, but people were looking for him and he'd be home soon.

A half-truth to be sure, but an age-appropriate one. Jarrah obviously internalised a lot more than his family realised so they hadn't wanted to keep him out of the loop but they hadn't wanted to worry him either. There were enough people in the house doing that, including Wally, who had taken up position on the floor in front of Jarrah.

As time dragged, a hard lump of nerves knotted and looped in Harper's belly. Waves of nausea came and went as Harper entreated the universe.

Please let him be alive. Please let him be all right. Please don't let him die.

She didn't really believe in any kind of divine influence but, in this moment, it felt as if she was at least doing something. Her only bright spot was that Ali was absolutely certain her brother was still alive and that gave her *hope*.

'Jarrah, why don't you get Vi and show Harper how big she is now?' Lyn suggested.

'Oh, yeah!' Jarrah leapt up and careened down the hallway, Wally close on his heels.

Harper raised an eyebrow at Ali. 'Vi?'

'The African violet.'

'Ah.'

Jarrah was back in seconds and, much to Harper's astonishment, he climbed right into her lap, settling there as he presented the terrarium. 'See, Harper? Vi's gots five flowers now.'

'Four,' Ali corrected with a laugh.

Wow...' Harper said automatically but the truth was there could have been two dozen flowers and it probably wouldn't have registered. She was still getting over the emotional whammy of Yarran's son crawling into her lap. He'd been great with her at his party but there was an easy, familiar intimacy to this action that stole her breath.

As if she was one of the family.

Harper wanted that desperately, she realised as she gazed down at the curly hair, so like his father's. Twelve years ago, the mere thought had terrified her, now she wanted *more* for herself. She wanted to grab the chance.

Of course, given how cold she'd been during their last conversation, Yarran might not want to give her that chance. Hell, he might not make it home.

She scrubbed the thought from her brain but when Jarrah turned his face up, looked at her intently and asked, 'Is my daddy going to be okay?' it pushed the thought front and centre again.

Harper's breath caught in her throat. The

enquiry was innocent enough but those dark eyes—Yarran's eyes—stared back at her with a heart-wrenching solemnity. Quite why he'd asked her, Harper wasn't sure. He'd have been better to ask Ali, whose twin ESP was keeping them all a little buoyed. But this was a little boy who'd already lost one parent and was obviously seeking reassurance.

And he'd chosen her.

'Absolutely.'

She remembered being shocked at Yarran's sweeping statement of assurance when Jarrah had been crying hysterically last Sunday. She'd never had anything sugar-coated in her life and it had felt wrong for Yarran to do that. But she *got* it now. There was time for brutal truths and time to give the gift of hope—false or not— because it was only human to want to hold onto the positive in any situation and, as a parent, sometimes, that was the job.

And in this moment, she would do anything, *say* anything, to allay the fears she could see lurking in Jarrah's dark expressive eyes.

'Your dad is smart and brave and *very* good at his job. He's going to be just fine.'

'Do you promise, Harper?'

She swallowed, the look of complete trust in his gaze more than she could bear. 'I promise.' And she hoped like hell it was true.

Come home, Yarran. Come home.

Coen's phone rang into the charged silence and Harper swore she could hear a collective intake of breath as he stood and answered. Lyn and Ali also both stood and hovered as Coen said, 'Yes, this is he…' And then, 'Yes…yes… Oh, *thank you*—' He huffed out a huge sigh and Ali and her mother embraced. 'That is good news. *Thank you.*'

Harper's breath released in a rush and she swallowed back against a surge of threatening bile as all the fears she hadn't dared give free rein suddenly flew away like dandelion puffs, leaving her light and airy and utterly elated.

'They found him. He's fine,' Coen confirmed as he placed the phone down, grinning from ear to ear. 'Concussed but otherwise uninjured. They're taking him to the Central.'

Jarrah's little face lit up in wonder as he turned his eyes on Harper. 'See,' she said with a huge smile. 'What did I tell you?'

Then he threw his little arms around her neck and hugged her and Harper knew, in that moment, she would do anything—*anything*—for this little boy.

Yarran slept heavily for he didn't know how long. Time was an unreliable narrator as he opened and closed his eyes, squinting against lights that were too bright and wincing at pain that was too damn much. His head thumped as flashes of memory chased each other in a foggy kind of never-ending dream.

A falling branch, the smell of burning and the aroma of eucalypts and a loamy forest floor. The scratch of dry leaves on his cheek. Then a siren and long corridors, things that beeped, the feel of crisp bedsheets and the smell of disinfectant and laundry detergent. Voices and faces, some he didn't know, others he did. His family—Jarrah and Ali and his parents. His other siblings.

And Harper. Who he loved. Harper, who didn't want to see him again.

More pain, grimacing at its intensity, wanting to tear his head from his shoulders, followed by periods of floating and the cool bliss of sleep.

Before it started all over again.

Then suddenly he broke through all the sluggishness weighing down his eyelids and he was awake. *Very* awake. Blinking at the bright lights and a *very* white ceiling. Not his bedroom. Way too white and...clinical. But the pain was much better, more like a dull backbeat than the symphony of pickaxes that had been chipping away at his skull.

Discombobulated, he just lay there for a moment, staring, trying to orientate himself and place the low *beep, beep, beep* he could hear somewhere off to the side. As he slowly turned his head to try and locate the noise, his eyes fell on a big chair beside his bed. Some kind of recliner, although the occupants were curled up on it rather than stretched out.

Harper. *And Jarrah.* Snuggled up together fast asleep. Jarrah hugging his…terrarium? Was he still dreaming? If he was, he didn't want to wake up.

A sudden prickle of moisture stabbed at his eyes and he had to shut them because it hurt too much. His eyes and his damn stupid heart. He opened them again, half expecting the apparition to be gone, but there they were. His two people. The little boy who'd become his whole world and the woman he'd loved for ever.

Yarran could hear the beeps getting faster, which instantly roused Harper, whose eyes flew in the direction of the beeping before cutting quickly to him, their gazes meshing. She was startled for a fraction of a second then almost fell out of the chair as she lurched quickly forward while trying to balance Jarrah.

'Yarran?'

'Hey,' he said, his voice croaky, his mouth dry as dirt and just as tasty.

Harper's moving had disturbed Jarrah. His eyelids fluttered a couple of times before opening then widening. *'Daddy?'* He glanced at

Harper with huge eyes. 'Is Daddy awake now like you said he would be?'

She beamed down at him. 'Yes, buddy, he is.'

Then they were both off the chair, crossing to him, and his heart was so damn full he thought it might explode. He didn't know how they'd got here—everything was fuzzy and it hurt to think too hard—but Harper was here—here with Jarrah—and it was all he cared about.

Harper helped Jarrah up on the bed. 'Be careful,' she said. 'Daddy's going to be sore and sleepy for a while so you have to be very gentle with him.'

Weak as a kitten, Yarran lifted his arm, encumbered by a drip. Jarrah slipped in beside him and kissed him on the shoulder with such sweet tenderness, Yarran wanted nothing more than to wrap him up in a huge hug. But everywhere, it seemed, there were drips and wires and bandages and he felt utterly feeble.

'We were scared, Daddy,' Jarrah whispered suddenly. 'Weren't we, Harper?'

She smiled and stroked Jarrah's head as she looked at Yarran. 'Yes, we were.'

Yarran held her gaze for long moments, reaching for her hand and holding it against his cheek. 'How long have I been sleeping for?'

'Two days.'

Yarran blinked. 'Bloody hell.'

'Oops, Daddy did a swearsy,' Jarrah said, laughing in delight.

Harper laughed too, as did Yarran despite how much it hurt. Her hand stroked his head, her fingers pushing into his hair, and he shut his eyes, it felt so good.

'How's your headache?'

He grimaced. 'It's there. But not like it has been.'

Suddenly the door opened and a nurse entered, followed by his parents and Ali as well as Brock and Riggs, and it was all kinds of pandemonium as everyone talked at once and there were tears and laughter and hugs galore and a hundred questions were answered and gaps were filled in and a doctor came and chatted about how lucky he was to escape with some superficial burns to his forehead and a mild concussion.

Yarran had to wonder, if this was mild, what a major case of concussion felt like because his exhaustion was brutal. Less than an hour later he was yawning as if it were an Olympic sport and he were going for gold. His nurse—bless her cotton socks—called time.

'Okay, everyone. Yarran needs to rest now.'

Harper agreed and everyone was dutifully shooed out. 'C'mon, you,' Ali said to Jarrah. 'You too.'

'But I wants to stays with Harper and Daddy.'

'He's okay,' Yarran said.

Harper glanced between him and Ali then back to him briefly before turning to Jarrah. 'Did you know the hospital has a garden on the roof?'

Jarrah gasped. 'Really, Harper?'

Yarran laughed. He wasn't sure when in the last couple of days Jarrah had started deferring to Harper, but he liked it.

'Yep. Really. It's my favourite spot.'

'How about we check it out?' Ali suggested. 'Then I'll bring you back to Daddy.'

'Okay.' Jarrah slipped his hand into his aunty Li-Li's and they headed for the door.

'Mmm.' Yarran shut his eyes as they departed and peace descended, the thump of his head lessening several degrees. 'I never noticed how loud they all were before.'

Harper laughed. 'I did.' He flicked his eyes open in time to see her face getting closer and closer, her forehead coming to rest on his cheekbone, her lips near his ear. 'You scared the living daylights out of me, Yarran Edwards. Don't ever do that again.'

Yarran smiled. 'No, ma'am.'

She kissed his cheek then and whispered, 'I love you.' Then she kissed all over his face whispering those three little words.

I love you.

'You do, huh?' he murmured as she brushed her mouth against the corner of his mouth. His tired body wasn't so tired suddenly.

She pulled back a little and nodded. 'I do. I know I said I didn't want to see you again but I was terrified I'd screwed up after everything was such a mess with Jarrah that day. And I figured that was fine because I hadn't even been back a month and it was too early for feelings. But I was with Ali when she got the call about you going missing and I felt physically ill thinking about you out there…injured, alone or *worse*…' She shuddered. 'And I knew that I loved you. I knew I'd never stopped.'

'When I opened my eyes and saw you and Jarrah snuggled up asleep before…' Yarran ran a finger down the side of her face, pushing a strand of red hair that had fallen forward back behind her ear '… I thought I must be hallucinating.'

'Not hallucinating. We've been clinging to each other for two days. I think maybe deep down we hoped you'd feel our combined love pulling you through.'

'I think maybe I did.' He smiled and even that hurt. 'Thank you. Thank you for being there for him while I've been like this. It means the world to me.'

In fact, he loved her for it. *He loved Harper*

Jones. For a lot of reasons, but for Jarrah in particular. Love multiplies, his mother had said, and she was right if the love trebling in his heart right now was any indication. It was so full it was fit to burst.

'*You* mean the world to me.'

She smiled tentatively. 'I do?'

'You do. I've just been guarding my heart for so long now, too frightened to risk it for me *and* for Jarrah. But the truth is I never fell out of love with you, either. Then I met Marnie and the love I felt for you became this thing in my past. But it didn't go. It was still there, it just… existed in a different time zone. And now here you are again and this love has bubbled back up whether I wanted it to or not because it's too strong to deny and it's made me feel whole again after feeling broken for the last three years.'

'Oh, *Yarran.*' She kissed him then, lightly, gently. 'You and Jarrah and coming back into your family has made *me* feel whole again. I used to feel what we had couldn't be real. Not for the likes of me. But I've never felt more whole than when I was with you and I want that again if you and Jarrah will have me.'

You and Jarrah. As far as three little words went—they were corkers.

'Except I'm going to trust it this time.' Her green eyes blazed sincerity. 'Trust you. Trust *us.*'

'Yes.' Yarran's fingers trembled as he pushed them into her hair. He'd never thought he'd have a second time around with his first love, but here she was, and he wanted nothing more than to spend the rest of his life with her and Jarrah as a family. 'Yes. We'll have you.'

He kissed her then, not gentle but with a hunger and desperation he could finally give free rein, his blood pressure spiking, heat flooding his groin. Until he hit her in the head with his IV tubing and a solar flare from the centre of his headache jabbed him straight through the eye.

He grunted as he broke off their lip lock. 'Okay…this might have to wait though,' he said on a half-laugh.

She laughed too and it sang in his blood. 'It's okay.' She smiled at him, stroking her cool fingers over the throb at his temple. 'I can wait.'

'Yeah.' Yarran smiled. He could too.

They had forever.

EPILOGUE

Two weeks later...

HARPER WAS NERVOUS. Her pulse fluttered madly at her temples. She couldn't believe she was about to *go there*. It had only been two weeks since Yarran had woken in his hospital bed and apart from the odd headache and still being on medical leave, he was back to normal.

But, if the incident had taught her anything, it was to make the most of every moment.

She knew intimately that no one was guaranteed happiness in life but falling for Yarran all over again had given her the courage to take it anyway. Realising that she *deserved* to be happy had come to her late in life—thanks to Yarran— and she didn't want to waste another moment.

'Hello? Earth to Harper?'

Harper tuned back into the conversation. They were at a table on the lower concourse of

Bennelong Point again, the sails of the Opera House glowing white in the background.

'Sorry… I was…'

What? Thinking something so ridiculous he might reject her outright?

Yarran leaned forward, his hand sliding over hers. 'Okay, what's up? You're acting funny. What's going on?'

She shook her head. 'It's fine. I'm fine.'

'Harper…'

He clearly wasn't convinced, and Harper knew it was now or never. She'd spent a lifetime not thinking she was worthy of love or happiness but the last two weeks with Yarran and Jarrah had given her courage.

Taking a deep breath, she eyeballed him. 'Okay… I'm about to float something so crazy I wouldn't blame you if you wanted to run a million miles away but, please, just let me get it out because I don't know if I'll ever be this brave again.'

He smiled that gentle smile of his and squeezed her hand. 'Okay.'

Harper took a breath. And then another, trying to quell the beat of her heart. 'Twelve years ago, you asked me to marry you and I wasn't ready. But I am now. And I know it's only been two weeks and we have to take it slow because we have Jarrah to consider and I have *no* issues with that. But I need you to know that I'm totally, absolutely, *utterly* in love with you. More than the first time around if that's even possible. And I never want to be with anyone but you and Jarrah and, when you're both ready, I'd like to walk down an aisle and have you *both* waiting for me down the other end.'

He blinked and Harper suffered a moment of panic. She'd gone too hard, too fast. But then common sense took over. Yarran loved her. She knew that. He was just going to need a minute, considering she'd been Little Miss Commitmentphobe.

'I'm sorry.' She grasped his fingers. 'I know it's a lot. Maybe too much, too soon.'

'No.' He shook his head, smiling in a way that sent her heart into a flutter. 'I've wanted to marry you since the moment I met you. It's not too much or too soon.'

He couldn't have chosen more perfect words. And when he leaned in and kissed her, his lips hot and needy, she believed him. She felt the usual tug at their contact but she knew—despite the yumminess of his kisses—this wasn't the moment for heated passion.

It was the moment for cool heads.

Pulling away, she pressed her forehead against his. 'Let's not make this a thing right now. We won't make it official. Let's be guided by Jarrah and where he's at.'

Yarran nodded, his smile sweet. 'Thank you. That means a lot to me. And we will be guided by Jarrah absolutely. But if you think I'm not going to want you as my wife every single day between now and then, you are seriously underestimating how much I want you by my side.'

'Oh, I think I know,' Harper murmured, her heart alive with the passion of his commitment.

He grinned. 'Oh, yeah? How much do you know?'

She produced a hotel room key, sliding it across the table. 'Five minutes away.'

He smiled a smile that flared an inferno in her underwear. 'Are you trying to seduce me, Jones?'

'Yes. Is it working?'

He caught the eye of a waiter. 'Cheque?' he said, and Harper smiled.

* * * * *

Look out for the next story in the
A Sydney Central Reunion quartet

Ivy's Fling with the Surgeon
by Louisa George

If you enjoyed this story, check out these
other great reads from Amy Andrews

Nurse's Outback Temptation
Tempted by Mr. Off-Limits
A Christmas Miracle

All available now!